SPARKS IN SCOTLAND

Also in the Flirt series:

SPARKS IN SCOTLAND

A. DESTINY AND RHONDA HELMS

SIMON PULSE

NEW YORK   LONDON   TORONTO   SYDNEY   NEW DELHI

SIMON PULSE
An imprint of Simon & Schuster Children's Publishing Division
1230 Avenue of the Americas, New York, New York 10020
First Simon Pulse paperback edition May 2015
Text copyright © 2015 by Simon & Schuster, Inc.
Cover photograph copyright © 2015 by Cultura/Paul Simon/Getty Images
All rights reserved, including the right of reproduction in whole or in part in any form.
SIMON PULSE and colophon are registered trademarks of Simon & Schuster, Inc.
For information about special discounts for bulk purchases, please contact
Simon & Schuster Special Sales at 1-866-506-1949 or business@simonandschuster.com.
The Simon & Schuster Speakers Bureau can bring authors to your live event. For more information or to book an event contact the Simon & Schuster Speakers Bureau at
1-866-248-3049 or visit our website at www.simonspeakers.com.
Designed by Regina Flath
The text of this book was set in Adobe Caslon Pro.
Manufactured in the United States of America
10 9 8 7 6 5 4 3 2 1
Library of Congress Cataloging-in-Publication Data
Destiny, A.
Sparks in Scotland / A. Destiny and Rhonda Helms. —First Simon Pulse paperback edition.
pages cm
Summary: While vacationing in Scotland with her parents, Ava, fifteen, meets cute and sweet Graham, the son of her mother's college friend, but wonders if it is worth pursuing a relationship when she will soon return to Cleveland.
[1. Vacations—Fiction. 2. Dating (Social customs)—Fiction. 3. Family life—Fiction. 4. Scotland—Fiction.] I. Helms, Rhonda. II. Title.
PZ7.D475Sp 2015
[Fic]—dc23
2014022116
ISBN 978-1-4814-2121-8 (pbk)
ISBN 978-1-4814-2123-2 (eBook)

SPARKS IN SCOTLAND

Chapter ❤ One

My entire body ached as I stretched each limb and popped my back, trying to shake off the effects of the long, long trip. Cleveland to New York to London to here—I still couldn't believe we'd left home yesterday afternoon and had just arrived in Edinburgh's airport a couple of hours ago.

But as I stared out our hotel window overlooking Princes Street, with Scotland's rolling greens and ancient buildings staring back at me, the stiffness in my body faded away. I was really here. And it was breathtaking so far. I couldn't wait to see what other sights Scotland held.

There was a lovely park area in front of our hotel with rich green grasses and trees, and beyond the park there were rows of ancient-looking buildings lined along the street, pressed side by side with pubs, shops, and churches. This whole city was steeped in history. I was crazy excited to explore.

My mom stepped behind me and gave a soft sigh. "It's gorgeous, isn't it?"

I nodded my agreement. "Well worth being cramped in an airplane for this." I'd spent hours last week scouring online to find pictures, videos, anything to help get me ready for our two-week vacation to Scotland. But nothing could have prepared me for the image before me.

Downtown Edinburgh bustled with people below, and music and noise filtered up to us from the packed streets. I couldn't help but smile as I watched. Excitement swelled, and I was suddenly itching to get out there and walk. I wanted to touch the warm bricks with my fingers, smell the pub food and flowers, and hear the noises up close and personal.

"Ava," my dad said from behind me, "I printed you a copy of our itinerary. There's also a backup on your bedside table."

Mom chuckled, and we turned and faced my dad. He didn't show any signs of fatigue, since he'd slept like a log on our flight from New York to London last night. I, on the other hand, had gotten intermittent sleep, due to the snoring man on my right who apparently couldn't snooze unless his head was tilted my way.

Mom and I sat down on my bed, and we dutifully took our copies of the papers while Dad recited an overall rundown of how the trip would go. First we would spend a few days in Edinburgh and the surrounding cities, and Dad would spend some of that time doing research on our family heritage. Then we were taking a weeklong bus trip through Oban, Inverness, and St. Andrews so we could explore the Scottish Highlands.

The more he talked, the more excited he got, his eyes flashing bright.

"And if we stick to this schedule, we'll have plenty of time to fit in almost everything the experts agree we need to see," he concluded with a flourish. "We'll experience a good portion of what Scotland has to offer."

"This sounds like a pretty thorough sightseeing plan you've crafted. But do we get to sleep anytime in there?" Mom asked, her lips quirking with quiet amusement. "And maybe have a dinner or two as well?"

He rolled his eyes. "Don't be ridiculous. Of course we do. I scheduled an hour for each meal—it's listed clearly under each day."

An hour? Yeah, right. Mom was the slowest eater in the world. Apparently, he'd forgotten about this little fact. "Good luck policing Mom's eating speed," I told him with a hearty chuckle.

She shot me a mock glare, then grabbed her phone. Her fingers flew over the screen as she typed. "Laugh it up, smarty-pants. I just believe in savoring my meals. Anyway, I'm sending Mollie a text to let her know we've arrived. I'm so excited to see her. It's been far too many years since she and I have hung out."

During our travels here, Mom had given me some information about this family we were hanging out with in Scotland.

Apparently, Mom and Mollie had been best friends in high school. After they'd graduated and moved on to college, Mollie had spent a semester in Scotland her senior year. She'd fallen head over heels in love—both with the land and with a handsome guy she'd met on campus. The decision to stay here had been hard, but she hadn't looked back.

Mollie's family still lived in the Cleveland area, and Mom said she had coffee with her parents every once in a while. But Mollie herself hadn't been back to visit in years.

The way Mom talked about Mollie reminded me of my friendship with Corinne. Lasting and strong, no matter what happened in life. We'd known each other for years and had grown into best friends fast. Before I'd left for this vacation, she'd demanded I send her lots of pictures of my trip and keep her up to date on all the cute guys I saw. If only she could have come with me to experience Scotland too. She would love what I'd seen so far; the old buildings and rolling greens would appeal to her artistic nature. Talk about inspiration.

"So, Dad, where are you going to start your research?" I asked. He'd joined an ancestry website last year to begin building our family tree, and it was cool to see the old scanned birth certificates, pictures, and other artifacts regarding our ancestors.

"The National Archives of Scotland." He dug through his suitcase and produced a battered notebook. As he flipped through the pages, I saw his signature scrawl filling at least the first half of the notebook. Dad was nothing if not thorough and methodical.

"It'll get me a good start on which town we should narrow our focus down to. And someone online mentioned I can check out local churches as well, since they keep meticulous birth and death records."

After interviewing a number of family members and confirming the information online, Dad had traced our family line back to Scotland. When he'd casually brought up the idea of continuing his research in person, Mom and I had begged him for a family trip there until he'd caved. We'd all figuratively tightened our belts and cut back on spending to make sure we could afford it, with no complaints.

Yeah, I was willing to follow any goofy, overplanned agenda Dad set if it meant experiencing this. Even our hotel felt cool and different and older than anything I'd seen in America. This country breathed history, and I was full of anticipation to take pictures and draw it.

"Will we be able to find out our family tartan?" I asked him. It would be so cool to get a kilt made in it. Corinne would die of jealousy if I wore it to visit her—and probably tease me a little too.

He shrugged. "If we have one, I don't see why not. I don't think all Scottish families do, but maybe we'll be lucky."

My stomach growled, and I clapped my hands over it with a chagrined laugh. "Sorry."

Mom quirked her crooked smile and put her phone away. "Someone's hungry, it seems."

"Well, it has been a few hours since we ate lunch," I protested.

And even that had been a little lackluster—a plain sandwich and chips. I wanted a real dinner.

Dad scrunched up his mouth as he thought. "Well, we're not actually scheduled to start exploring Edinburgh until tomorrow, but I suppose we could get a taste of its foods right now and maybe do a little shopping—"

"Yes!" Mom and I said together, then laughed. We jumped off the bed and stood in front of Dad with pleading eyes.

He gave a heavy, resigned sigh. "Okay, fine. Put on your jackets, and let's go grab a meal. There's a place on High Street that was recommended by a number of people. We'll get some authentic Scottish cuisine there."

I slipped on my dark-blue fleece jacket and checked myself out in the mirror. My blond bob was a bit worse for wear but not horribly so, and a quick run-through of my brush smoothed the strays. I had on jeans and a T-shirt. Not my foxiest outfit ever, but it would do for now.

"You look lovely, Ava," Mom said as she walked by me, giving my upper arm a small squeeze.

We left the room and made our way down the hall, down the stairs, and into the large wood-trimmed lobby. A variety of people hustled and bustled around us, checking in as they dragged suitcases to the front desk, talking, laughing. Their energy was infectious, and I found my spirits lifted even higher.

Wow, I was in Scotland—I was really here! And this was going to be an awesome two weeks.

"Oh, just to remind you," Mom said to me when we stepped outside into the mild summer air. "Mollie and Steaphan have a son around your age. Graham. He'll be hanging out with us too," she added with a broad smile.

My good mood slipped a touch, and a hint of wariness filled me. Wonderful. Mom's attempts at vacation matchmaking weren't very subtle.

We crossed Princes Street and headed down the sidewalk toward High Street, weaving through the crowds of people. The air carried the rich scents of food and the sounds of drummers off in the distance. Sunlight peeked through intermittent clouds and warmed the air, which hovered around the midsixties. When we'd left Cleveland yesterday, it had been in the nineties and scorching hot for days. This was far, far more comfortable.

"I'm sure Graham is a nice guy," I finally said to Mom. My stomach growled again. I focused on my hunger in an attempt to change the subject. "So, I can't wait to try this restaurant. Do you think you'll try haggis while we're here? I don't know if I'm brave enough to eat it."

Mom ignored my food ramblings and continued, "You should give him a chance, Ava. I've seen Graham's pictures, and he's quite handsome. A clean-cut boy with a friendly smile."

"I'm sure he is." I knew the grin on my face was super fake, but I flashed it anyway. A mother's idea of handsome was quite different from a daughter's. Plus, I tended to like guys who were a little less prim and proper. David's short, scruffy black hair and dark-brown eyes came to mind, and I shoved the memory right back out again. At least that old sting in my heart didn't flare up at the thought of him, the way it had for so long after our breakup earlier this year.

Dad, who was already in tourist mode, had his camera at the ready and was busy snapping shots of the large brick and stone buildings lining the street. I took out my phone and snapped a few shots so I could send them to Corinne.

Mom nudged me with her shoulder and gave me a wistful smile. She was such a romantic. "I know what you're thinking, Ava, but who knows? Graham might turn out to be your Scottish vacation romance. After all, Mollie hadn't planned on falling in love, but here she is, almost twenty years later and still happy as a lark."

I gave her a casual shrug. Yeah, it would be awesome to find someone I liked that much, but I wouldn't hold my breath. I'd liked David too, a lot, and that had turned out terribly. No one else knew what had happened between us to make us break up, not even Corinne, and I wanted to keep it that way. The truth was far too mortifying. "We'll see," I replied with a broad smile. "I'm looking forward to meeting them all." That much was accurate, at least.

We turned the corner and headed down High Street. I couldn't stop staring, absorbing the sights of Old Town Edinburgh. The buildings were packed side by side with adorable storefronts in brilliant colors. Rich Scottish accents poured from young and old guys sitting at pub tables as they talked faster than I could understand, pints in hand. Everywhere I looked I saw tartan patterns on clothing and even a few men in kilts. Their bare calves were strong and sturdy, covered with hair.

A couple of blocks down, Dad led us into a small restaurant with huge glass windows. A waitress with wildly curly gray hair and a warm face seated us and gave us menus. I scoured mine a little hesitantly at first but realized I recognized a lot of the food available and felt a strong sense of relief. An embarrassed flush crept up my cheeks. If my mom could read my thoughts right now, she'd make a pointed comment about me always making assumptions.

Mom and Dad ordered, and I got the sausage-and-mash bake—couldn't go wrong with potatoes and sausage. My parents talked about tomorrow's plans with Mollie and Steaphan, and I let my gaze wander around the room. The top half was blue wallpaper, while the bottom was wood-trimmed with neat tables lined up along the walls. It was cozy and lovely.

And the air smelled heavenly. I couldn't wait to eat.

"—excited to find out where we're really from," Dad was saying. "I should be able to search all the way back to our home village, even." He suspected our heritage could be traced way back to the medieval ages, based on something he'd found online, and was hoping to confirm it with in-person research.

Our meals were delivered fast, and the food was every bit as good as I'd hoped it would be. I polished off my whole plate in record time. My parents got fish and fries—uh, chips, as our waitress called them.

We paid our bill and left the restaurant, then spent a couple of hours strolling along High Street to window-shop a bit. I was tempted to buy a bunch of stuff, but I didn't want to spend all my money on the first day.

The temperature had dropped a few degrees, and I zipped my fleece up a touch. Crazy how much hotter Ohio was than Scotland. Good thing Mom and I had done our research beforehand and had packed appropriate clothing.

As the sun began to sink into the horizon, we made our way back to our hotel. My eyes were gritty and I was a bit sluggish. Mom was walking slower too, and even Dad's enthusiasm was starting to fade. Fatigue definitely hit us hard after that big meal.

Still, I wasn't quite ready to go to sleep yet. When we got inside, I begged to explore the hotel a bit. Mom and Dad reluctantly agreed. I grabbed a room key and took off before they could change their mind.

The building was old, and all its little details mesmerized me as I walked up and down the halls, trailing my fingers along the walls. Spindly metal wall sconces glowed with golden lamplight. Ornate wallpaper covered the halls in subtle patterns I could feel under my fingertips, and the carpeted halls were worn but soft. I was tempted to kick off my shoes and dig my toes in the plush brown nap.

There were a few modern, updated rooms in the hotel's first floor as well, for business conferences, I assumed, bearing massive slabs of tables and sleek chairs. The dining hall was a large, blue-carpeted room with dark wooden tables in intimate clusters and small candles in the center of each smooth surface. The space invited people to come in and linger for a while. I needed to ask Mom and Dad if we could eat there tomorrow. Even though I was full, the rich scents of cooking food from the nearby kitchen tempted me to eat more.

When I got back to the lobby, I noticed a group of guys standing together. There was a mix of accents tangling—Irish, English, even German. One English guy had a shock of blond hair and stood a good foot taller than the rest. Super handsome. It was so tempting to take a quick picture to send to Corinne, but I didn't want to look too obvious. I made a mental note to tell her about it.

I headed upstairs, tiptoed into the room—my folks were already asleep—got ready for bed, then conked out almost before my head hit the pillow.

Chapter ● Two

Saturday morning I slowly woke from a much-needed deep sleep. As I blinked the drowsiness out of my eyes and looked around the room, for a moment I wasn't sure where I was. Then I remembered. We were in Scotland, and it was our first full day of vacation. A giddy smile swept over my face, and I hopped out of bed.

Mom groaned and shoved the pillow over her face from her bed. "So. Early," she mumbled.

I chuckled. She never was much of a morning person, but I'd gotten a full night's sleep, and I was ready to explore Edinburgh. "You'll feel better once you get coffee in your system," I told her.

"Your father already went downstairs to get me some," she said with a sleepy smile. "I love that man."

Dad's laptop was open and ready with the messenger box

active—I'd asked him yesterday if I could use the computer to talk to Corinne this morning—so I fired off a quick message to Corinne just to say hi, along with a picture I'd taken of High Street yesterday. Then I hopped in the shower and got dressed. My skinny jeans made me feel confident, and I paired them with a bright red long-sleeved shirt.

I took a few extra minutes to do my hair and makeup before I proclaimed myself ready. By then, Dad had returned and Mom had begun her waking-up process. It was so hard not to nudge them to move faster; I was eager to get going.

An hour later we had grabbed a quick breakfast and were finally walking down the Royal Mile, a stretch of street that ran between the queen's palace and Edinburgh Castle. The morning sky was patchy with clouds, and the air was fairly brisk, but people seemed in good spirits as they wandered up and down the sidewalks. The storefronts along the Royal Mile beckoned me with souvenirs, tempting smells, eye-catching tartans.

What would it be like to live here? They had to get visitors from all over the world. It would be so fun to have a small art gallery along this street. I could put up my art and Corinne's, and—

"—tour the castle with Mollie and Graham," Mom was saying, "and your father will hit the National Archives with Steaphan. Sound good?"

I nodded my agreement. Whoops. I needed to pay better attention instead of letting my mind wander.

We reached the outskirts of the castle and stood off to the

side while small tourist groups filtered in, headed by enthusiastic tour guides wearing tartan-patterned vests and pants. Excitement buzzed in my veins; I was so ready to get started poking around the castle. Part of me was also a little nervous about meeting Mollie and her family. Okay, about meeting Graham.

"Oh, there she is!" Mom said as she gave a hearty wave over her head.

I watched a black-haired woman my mom's age make her way toward us, her hand threaded through a tall and slender man's fingers. To her other side was a guy—I assumed it was her son. My immediate reaction was to suck in a rapid shock of air.

Graham was attractive.

Really attractive.

Wow. Mom hadn't been kidding. The guy's dark hair was clipped close, but was wavy enough that it wouldn't lie totally flat. His eyes were shocking blue and flashed brightly in the glints of sunlight peeking through the clouds. He was tall like his father, lean, and his hands were tucked casually in his jacket pockets. His jacket was black, which made his black hair and blue eyes even more noticeable.

When the family neared us, I swallowed and crossed my arms over my chest. Then dropped my hands and propped one on my hip. Then dropped that hand too. Good grief, I felt awkward and dorky compared to his effortless movements.

His mom beamed at my mom, then rushed over to give her a hug. "Oh my God!" the woman said in a bubbly tone as they squeezed each other. "I missed you so much! I can't believe you're here. I feel like I've been waiting forever for this." When she pulled back, there were tears in her eyes.

I couldn't help but smile at the warmth between the two women. My mom's eyes glistened with tears too, and she gushed to Mollie about how beautiful Scotland was and what our trip here had been like.

Dad stuck out his hand to Steaphan, and the two men introduced themselves. Then Steaphan introduced himself to me and waved Graham over.

"Good mornin'!" Steaphan said to me with a hearty smile. "Nice to meet ya! This here's my son, Graham."

My pulse thudded in my veins as I shook Graham's hand, which was warm and firm and so inviting. "Hi," I said.

He gave me a curt nod, then stepped away.

My stomach lurched at his abrupt response, but I made myself smile wider to cover my feelings. Okay then. Obviously Graham didn't want to be forced to hang out with me today. No biggie—I'd make sure to stay with our moms then. He could walk around by himself.

I shook off my frustration and turned to my mom. "Ready to go inside?" I asked her in a chipper voice. No way was I going to let this guy get to me.

She gave my dad a kiss on the cheek. "You men behave."

Dad shook his head as he chuckled, while Steaphan winked. Obviously the two would get along fine. They walked away, and our group of four strolled to the ticket line. Mom and Mollie were talking so fast it was almost dizzying. When was the last time I'd seen her this happy?

It made my heart feel a pang for Corinne. This was a country to be shared with someone you cared about. Not a stranger who didn't seem to think me worthy of even polite conversation. Corinne would have had something blunt to say about his attitude. That thought gave me a smile.

The stone walls everywhere were stunning. I took in the old buildings around us, the cobblestones on the ground. I snapped a shot of the castle grounds with my phone—I wasn't allowed to use it to send pictures, but I could upload them later and send in a chat.

"So, where to first?" Mom asked Mollie.

She shrugged, then turned to me. "What do you fancy looking at?"

I smiled. Her voice held a trace of Scottish accent and slang, even though she'd been an American for the first half of her life. "What if we just wander around and go into buildings as we get to them?"

Mom nodded, then threaded her arm through Mollie's, and they walked a few steps ahead of us. Graham fell into pace at my side, maintaining a polite distance between us. His body language was stiff, which made me feel awkward as well. Did he dislike all Americans, or was it just me?

We made our way into the heart of the castle grounds and looked at the exterior of the Governor's House, then popped into the National War Museum of Scotland.

"This place must be super old," I murmured to myself while I walked. There was a tour guide nearby talking with a small group, so I listened in as the guide pointed out the uniforms and weapons displayed and gave historical background on the battles they'd been used in.

Out of the corner of my eye I saw Graham walking along, examining each piece with studious care. The light in the building glinted in his dark hair. He really was attractive. Too bad he wasn't friendly at all.

He walked over to Mom and Mollie, and a brief but genuine smile creased his face, which made my heart stop in my chest for a moment. Wow. The gesture really transformed him from brooding and disinterested to engaging and magnetic.

Apparently it was just me he didn't want to talk to. But how could I have offended the guy before I'd even met him?

Maybe he'd gotten a negative first impression of me somehow. Had my mom told his mom something embarrassing or bad? Or was he ticked about being forced to hang out with me when he wanted to be somewhere else?

Whatever. I ripped my gaze away from them and went back to looking at the exhibits. This vacation wasn't about trying to get a guy to like me. It was about learning the ins and outs of Scotland. I wasn't going to get into that dating pattern again.

Already been there, done that, with David.

I bit back a sigh. David, my first real boyfriend, who'd captured my heart last year in an all-encompassing way. He sang with our high school's glee club, was creative like me, and was the life of every gathering. When we'd first started talking at a friend's birthday party, I'd been so flattered by his attention. He'd given me this broad, charming smile and told me I was the prettiest girl in the room.

And I'd eaten it up, hook, line, and sinker.

Our relationship had started so well, I never would have suspected it ending the way it had—with him dumping me so unceremoniously, saying in that cold voice that he'd never really liked me the way I'd liked him.

Mom and Mollie walked over toward me, whispering back and forth about the exhibits.

"It's sad how bloody and violent Scotland's history is," I heard Mom said quietly.

Mollie nodded. "One thing I've learned since living here is Scottish pride. Despite their war-torn past, the Scottish still believe in their country and are proud of their heritage."

"Da's drilled that into yer head," Graham said in a thick brogue as he moved beside his mom. He offered the two women a smile.

She laughed. "Yeah, your da isn't shy about expressing his love for his homeland."

"Mine isn't either," I said to her with a small chuckle. "He's always wanted to visit here. I think this trip will make him love Scotland even more, now that he has concrete evidence of our family's roots."

Graham's gaze drifted to mine, and he blinked, like he was actually seeing me for the first time, despite our earlier introduction. I stood there for a moment, our eyes locked. The guy was super intense, and despite my brain telling me I should look away, I couldn't.

From the corners of my eyes I could see Mom's smug smirk aimed in my direction, and she and Mollie walked off, their whispers fading.

My pulse thrummed in my throat as Graham took a step toward me. He stopped a couple of feet away, and I craned my head to stare up into his eyes.

His lips quirked in the corner. "Enjoyin' the artifacts?"

I nodded. I couldn't quite figure out what this guy's deal was, but at least he wasn't being a total snob now. "It's kind of dark and scary, but important."

"Wait till ya see the palace. The rooms are splendid."

We followed our moms through the rest of the war museum, then went back out into the fresh air. A strange tension crackled in the air between me and Graham, but it wasn't negative, like it had been earlier. Frankly, I was just glad he wasn't ignoring me anymore, if only because I didn't want to spend any more time today crabby and stressed about it.

I was pretty sure Mom and Mollie had been talking nonstop. When their giggles wafted back to us as we strolled past the Governor's House through Foog's Gate, Graham and I exchanged bemused smiles.

Weird parents—seemed like they could unite just about anyone.

He cleared his throat, and even in the dimmer light I could see his cheeks flush a dark pink. "Erm. Sorry 'bout earlier, Ava. Had a bit of a bad mornin'. Didn't mean to take it out on ya—wasn't fair of me."

Well, that was unexpected. I nodded as a slight weight lifted off my chest. "Thanks. I understand. Plus, I'm sure you had other things you wanted to do on your Saturday instead of spending it with your mom's American friends." Being forced into a social situation by parents was likely to make any teen frustrated and crabby.

"Nah, that wasn't it." An emotion flashed in his eyes but left before I could decipher it. "Been a while since I've played tourist around here, yanno. This is fun, and I'm glad I came."

I wanted to close my eyes and let the rich brogue of his voice wash over me. There was nothing quite like the sound of a Scottish guy talking. I almost laughed at myself for how ridiculous and moony-eyed I probably looked right now. I tilted my chin up and eyed him. "I haven't done a lot of tourist things in Cleveland, either," I admitted. "Somehow I just run out of time."

"Cleveland. Yer in Ohio, right?"

I nodded. "Lived there my whole life."

We headed to the terrace in front of St. Margaret's Chapel and turned to face the panoramic view of Edinburgh. I rested my hand on my chest and just stared in awe. Incredible. The hills rolled on as far as the eye could see, and Edinburgh's old buildings were scattered everywhere.

"There's nothing in Cleveland that compares to this," I proclaimed as I surveyed the city.

"Aye," he said, and I heard the pride in his tone. "She's a beautiful city." He looked down at me, and a breeze ruffled the tips of his hair. His eyes glowed a brilliant pale blue, and his face held a hint of a smile.

Oh wow. My heart almost stopped in my chest. There was something about Graham even beyond his attractiveness that made a girl want to fall into his eyes. He was intense, magnetic. My stomach squeezed in warning, and I swallowed and gave him a shaky smile in response.

Maybe spending the day with Graham wasn't going to be so bad after all.

Chapter ● Three

After the four of us peered around St. Margaret's Chapel, taking in the stunning stained-glass window, we popped back out and headed toward the Royal Palace. The rooms in here were quiet, humming with the soft whispers of visitors. Wood panels, thick stones, ornate paintings—the place was stunning. I couldn't get over how old everything was. What would it have been like to live in this palace?

"Take a look over there," Graham whispered to me with a nod of his head to my right.

I turned and looked . . . and saw the Crown Jewels. With a blink, I asked, "Is that really . . ."

He grinned, and his teeth flashed in the light. "Aye. The real deal."

The bejeweled crown was set on blue velvet, with a sword and a scepter presented around it. My fingers itched to pop it on my head, just to see what it felt like. With all the gold and jewels on it, it was probably heavy. But I didn't want to get kicked out of Scotland on my first full day.

"Whatcha smilin' about?" he asked, eyes twinkling with curiosity.

"Oh. Um, I was just thinking what it would be like to be royalty. We don't have anything like that in the States." Unless you counted movie stars or the president, I supposed. But there was something unique about a monarchy.

"So tell me about America." He slipped into an easy pace beside me, and his cologne wafted to my nostrils. His scent was light and fresh, drawing me closer.

My pulse picked up again, and I struggled to keep my voice even and not give away my attraction to him. "Um, what do you want to know?"

"Ya go to . . . high school—that's what it's called in America, right? What is that like?"

We walked into another room and eyed the paintings on the walls. A bunch of serious, severe-looking men and women frowned at us from their luxurious clothing and tapestries captured on the canvases.

"I just finished my sophomore year—I'll start eleventh grade in the fall." I tilted my head and studied the jewel-draped woman in front of me as I thought about how to describe American high school. "Basically, it's chaos," I said with a light laugh. "We have classes on many subjects, on many different levels, depending on where you placed—regular, honors, advanced. I don't have a lot of classes with my friends, but I can choose which kind of math or history or science I want to take, which is nice."

"What classes did ya take this year?"

I described my sophomore year schedule, including how I'd lucked out and got to take both art and photography. "So I was able to get out of study hall and do more art."

"I just finished my fourth year of secondary school," he told me. "From what I understand, our school systems are quite different. For us, secondary school starts when yer eleven or twelve, and ya go for up to six years."

"So you guys basically group middle school and high school together. Interesting." I'd never imagined how different school systems could be, depending on where you lived in the world.

We walked into the Great Hall, which was a large red and wood-trimmed room lined with swords and armor. It was massive and imposing, and I couldn't stop staring.

"Oh wow," I breathed. "This is gorgeous."

Mom pointed out a display case to Mollie, and they walked over to study it.

"So what do you do when you're not in school?" I asked him. What was life like for the average Scottish guy?

"Well, I put on a kilt and run through the Highlands as my friends and I dance to the bagpipes." His lips quirked as he stared at me with a lifted eyebrow.

I scrunched up my face in mock consternation. "Okay, you're putting me on." Though I had to admit, his comment drew a huff of laughter out of me.

"Maybe a wee bit," he admitted with a grin. "I go on my computer, talk to friends, play the drums—"

"Oh, you're a musician." My heart thunked. Stupid weakness of mine; I loved guys who were musically inclined. "I wish I could play something. I tried trumpet in middle school and I was awful."

"I started when I was a lad. Da taught me. I'm in a band, actually."

"That's so cool," I breathed. "What kind of music do you play? Do you do covers of songs or write original pieces?"

"We do both. I've written a couple of songs, but we also cover popular rock groups. We've played a few parties, that kind of thing. We have another gig in a few weeks, actually." I could hear the pride in his voice.

We walked in companionable silence for a moment. Wow. My first impression of Graham was nothing like how he really was. All his earlier attitude was gone—either he'd gotten over whatever had made him crabby, or he'd decided to let it go and try to enjoy the day.

We followed our moms and wandered around through the rest of the building, but I had to admit, the castle didn't hold as much of my interest as Graham did. As we walked, he offered commentary on a few of the portraits, relaying strange and quirky facts about the castle's inhabitants.

"How do you know so much?" I asked him.

His face was deadpan. "All Scots know these things."

"Really?" Wow, that put us Americans to shame. Probably half my friends couldn't tell me the names of the last five presidents.

He chuckled. "No, I'm teasing ya. My da—"

"Come on, guys," Mollie interrupted, reaching out to tug his hand. "You're dragging along, and we're hungry. Let's finish touring the castle and get something to eat on the Royal Mile. And kick up our feet for a bit too—mine are aching."

The rest of our tour went a little faster. We poked around the War Memorial and the Half Moon Battery, then left the castle. I'd gotten several good photographs I was happy with.

"That was incredible," I told Graham in a rush.

"'Twas," he agreed.

The sun was warm, so I stripped my fleece off and tied it around my waist. Graham's gaze raked over me, and then he quickly looked away. Luckily, he didn't see the flush crawl across my cheeks. I turned my attention to the Royal Mile, a long stretch of old buildings as far as the eye could see. It bustled with people walking to and fro.

A band of men wearing kilts and carrying tiny accordions went walking by, playing and singing loudly as they danced their way down the street. We cheered them on. A crowd of a dozen or so little kids followed behind, tiny hands clapping as they screamed for more music. One of the men, who had a huge mustache, shot me a bold wink as he passed, and Mom giggled as she elbowed me in the side.

"That's hilarious," I said, my stomach hurting from laughing so hard. "They looked like they were having a blast."

"Never know what yer gonna see here," Graham said with a grin.

Mom and Mollie stopped us at a pub with outdoor seating. We popped into the metal seats, and I sighed in relief to get off my aching feet for a few minutes. All that walking was adding up. The waitress, a young blonde in her twenties, came out and cheerfully took our sandwich orders. Graham's long legs were splayed under the glass-top table, and his knee brushed mine as he shifted in his seat.

I sucked in a shaky breath, torn between wanting to move my leg and wanting to push it closer to his. Good grief, this guy was causing some crazy, mixed-up reactions in me. And I'd practically just met him.

I cleared my throat. "So, Mom," I said in an effort to distract myself from his nearness, "tell me more about how you and Mollie met."

That worked. The two women talked over each other, spilling the story of their friendship. Apparently, they'd met back in elementary school when they'd been assigned to work at the same art station. When they'd both realized their favorite color was green, they'd become instant friends, the way little kids often bonded.

Our food was delivered, and we noshed as they continued to talk.

"Before the Internet, we would write letters back and forth," Mollie explained to me and Graham. "It was one of my favorite things back in those early days, getting a letter from your mom."

Mom's smile widened, and she reached over and squeezed

Mollie's hand. "Me too," she said with a slight sheen in her eyes. "Of course, now we have e-mail and chat messengers and texts and cell phones to help us talk. Gotta love technology."

My heart squeezed at the real, true friendship between them. Despite the distance, they'd made it work. It made me happy to see. Even Graham seemed touched, his eyes smiling as he looked quietly at them.

"Remember that time we both liked the same guy?" Mollie suddenly asked. She tilted her head in thought. "Um, his name was Bradley . . . Bradley . . ."

"Oh my God!" Mom said with a laugh. She clapped her hand over her mouth. "Bradley Amos? He was so cute. Remember those thick black glasses and how he'd look at us over the top of them?"

Graham raised an eyebrow at me, and I just shrugged. Our faces held matching smiles.

I finished my last bite and looked around the street. Now that I'd eaten and rested up, I wanted to explore more of the strip. It was tempting to ask Graham to join me, but I didn't want to assume anything. "Mom, can I walk around for a while?" I asked in a hesitant tone. "I'll stay right here on the Royal Mile, and I have my phone with me."

She looked uncertain. "I'm not sure I like the idea of you wandering around by yourself. . . ."

"I just want to do a little window-shopping. Pretty please." I clasped my hands in front of me and shot her my most begging look.

Her response was to narrow her eyes with a knowing smirk. "I know what you're trying to do, missy. But it's not safe, and you know I worry."

"I'd be happy to take her around if ya want," Graham offered. He wiped his hands on his napkin and plopped it beside his plate. When he glanced at me, there was a slight tinge of pink on his cheeks. "If she wants me to, that is. Wouldn't want to assume anything."

Was he nervous? The thought made my own pulse stutter in response. "Um, yeah. Of course. I'd like that."

Mom hesitated for a moment more, then looked at Mollie, who gave an encouraging nod. "Oh, I suppose. But only for a half hour or so, okay? And keep that phone in your pocket."

I jumped up, kissed her on the cheek, and said, "Thank you!"

Graham slid out of his seat and said good-bye to his mom. His smile was friendly as he neared me, and I suddenly found myself feeling awkward again. It was one thing to follow our moms around. Quite another for us to be alone.

I nibbled my lip as we made our way down the street, studying the tall, ancient buildings, their peaks climbing into the sky.

"Grand street, yeah?" he asked me in that compelling rumble of a voice.

I nodded. "I feel like I want to see everything all at once. It's so much to take in. So, where exactly do you live?"

"Not too far from here. A wee south."

Another small band strolled by, this one playing drums. A

crowd built along the street line, and we stopped and watched. The lead drummer, a man a little older than my dad, flipped his drumsticks in the air, and the crowd roared its approval.

"It isn't like this back home," I said as I clapped along with the music. "Our streets in Cleveland have nothing but traffic jams and grumpy drivers."

He chuckled. "We have our share of those as well." His fingers brushed my upper arm, and goose bumps rippled from the contact. When he gave me a warm smile, I felt something in my chest melt a little bit. "I have an idea of where we should go."

He took my hand to lead me through the crowd, and my lungs contracted to the size of grapes. All I could focus on was the feel of our bare skin touching. It was easy to get a sense of his strength from the firm grip, not to mention the slight calluses on his fingers—probably from playing drums.

We stopped in front of a light-blue store, and I gave out a squeal of excitement. "A tartan shop! Oh, how cool is that?"

His grin grew wider as he held the door open for me and ushered me inside. The bell rang when the door closed, and a portly bald man wearing a kilt came lumbering from the back.

"Welcome!" he cried out. "Can I give ya a hand?"

"Aye," Graham said. "My American friend here would like to try on a kilt, if it's all right?"

"Come with!" the man told me with a wave of his hand. He led me to an area in front of a three-way mirror. "Yer a right wee one, ain't ya!" At my blush, he laughed heartily and went to a shelf holding a bunch of folded tartan, then snagged a beautiful blue-and-green-plaid pattern.

His accent was heavy, but between him and Graham and their hand gestures, we managed to get the kilt wrapped around me and adjusted correctly. I still had my jeans on underneath, but I got the idea of how it would look.

"This is so cool," I said as the store owner helped me tuck the last bit in. I twirled in the mirror and admired the pleats in the back. "I'm definitely bringing my mom back here to buy me one." She'd already promised that once we found out our official family tartan, we'd get kilts made in it. And if we didn't have a tartan pattern, we'd just find one we liked and get those.

"Ye look Scottish-born," the store owner said as he nodded his approval.

"I love it so much. Thank you for showing me the proper way to wear it." I peeked at the time on my phone and frowned. "Darn, I have to go." I didn't want to make my mom mad on my first solo outing in Scotland. If I stuck to the rules she set now, odds were she'd be more flexible in the future.

Graham stepped forward to help me get out of the kilt. His fingers brushed my waist over the top of my shirt, and I saw the pulse at the base of his throat jump. He froze, looking down at me with that strange intensity of his. Then he blinked and stepped away, his cheeks flushed yet again. "Uh, sorry 'bout that."

My breath was too busy being locked in my lungs for me to

speak for a moment. Finally I forced a careless grin and said, "It's okay. I think the kilt hypnotized us all."

"That it did," he replied, his eyes dancing.

We both laughed, the mood lightened. But as we thanked the store owner and made our way to the pub to meet our moms, the cloud-dappled sky bold and bright overhead, I couldn't help but think about how much fun I was having with him so far.

And how it sure seemed like he was having fun with me too.

Chapter Four

Look at this!" I told Mom as I held up an oversize white coffee mug that said KISS ME, I PLAY THE BAGPIPES in big gold letters. "Wouldn't this be perfect for Corinne's dad?"

Mom laughed and nodded. "I think you're right. The man sure does drink a lot of coffee." A running joke between me and Corinne was that she was always being sent to the corner store to buy her dad another bag of coffee beans. Seemed like she was going once or twice a week at times.

We poked around the small tourist shop, and I checked the time on my phone for the two hundredth time this morning. Mom had told me when I'd gotten up that Graham and his family were going to hang out with us again today. They would meet us at the Palace of Holyroodhouse and spend the entire Sunday with us.

I'd given her a casual nod in response, but on the inside, my stomach had fluttered like crazy. It had been a long time since I'd found myself this attracted to a guy. Was Graham nervous to see me again too, or was this attraction one-sided?

I moved toward the postcard rack and flipped through the gorgeous images. Well, it didn't matter if this crush was one-sided or not. I was only in Scotland for two weeks. A lasting relationship couldn't be built on that.

Except . . . Mom and Mollie had maintained their friendship for years under those circumstances.

"Find anything for Corinne?" my dad asked. "Oh, that one is gorgeous." He pointed at a panoramic shot of Edinburgh on a sunny summer day.

I picked it up. "Yeah, she'd definitely like this." Corinne was a brilliant painter. Maybe I could get her to do something for me to help commemorate my trip. Nothing in this store seemed like the right gift for her, though. I'd have to keep looking.

"We should get going," Mom said as she checked her watch. "We don't want to be late meeting them."

That got my stomach tweaking again. I pressed a palm to my belly and drew in slow breaths. Last night I'd fallen asleep thinking about Graham's broad smile. I was pretty sure I'd woken up with a ridiculous grin plastered on my face. The guy was getting to me for sure.

I gave Mom a nod, then moved to the counter to make my purchases. All that babysitting I'd done over the year was coming in handy right now. It was nice having my own spending money.

"So what did you find in your research yesterday?" I asked Dad as we walked down the street toward the palace. "Anything interesting?"

He had his camera out and was snapping pictures, so our progress toward the palace was slow. "I was able to trace our lineage back even further than what I'd found online. And I'm pretty sure our ancestors lived near Glencoe."

"That's so cool. Can we check it out while we're here?"

"Absolutely. In fact, we're going to be in Glencoe on our bus tour," Dad said. He paused to line up the perfect shot of the buildings across the street. *Click.* "We'll be able to drop by and see if the local church has any records I can examine." He dropped his camera and looked at me and Mom, sheer bliss shining in his eyes. "How cool is it that we can do this? That I'm able to find these resources and discover who our ancestors were?"

"You're a regular Sherlock," I teased him.

He nudged me with his shoulder, then snapped a shot of my face. "Very funny, princess."

I walked between my parents, who talked nonstop about the sights and sounds around us. Even on a Sunday morning, Edinburgh bustled with tourists and others. This morning the sun was out in its full glory, the only clouds scattered far off in the horizon, and the temperature was in the upper sixties. I turned my face up to the sunshine and smiled.

We neared the palace, and my heart began that stutter-beat thing it did whenever I thought about Graham.

Mom shot me a knowing smile. "Someone looks really happy this morning."

I pretended like I didn't know what she meant and shot her a wide-eyed, innocent look. "Of course I'm happy. It's a gorgeous day out, and we're in Scotland."

"Uh-huh." Her grin grew wider. "I'm sure it has nothing to do with a certain attractive Scottish guy."

Dad stopped and stared hard at me. "What's this you're talking about? What guy? Do you mean Steaphan's kid?"

"He's not a kid" was on the tip of my tongue, but I didn't want him doing the Dad thing and griping at me about getting a crush on a local hottie. So I replied, "Graham and I walked around while Mom and Mollie spent all day giggling."

Mom gave a healthy snort. "I'll remember that when you have your next sleepover with Corinne."

We made it to the entrance of the castle and stood off to the side as we waited for our companions to show up. I smoothed my hair down and tucked the errant strands behind my ears. To distract myself, I checked out the three-story castle exterior, the sprawling green grounds.

"Can you believe how many castles there are even just in Edinburgh?" I asked my parents.

"You can't travel very far in Scotland without hitting a castle," Dad said with a chuckle. "Maybe when you get older, you can buy one. Oh, look—here they are."

Mollie and Steaphan strolled up to us with cheery waves.

"Good morning!" Mollie said. She turned to me. "You ready to do more exploring today?"

I nodded and tried not to stare at Graham as he neared. Today he had on a long-sleeved pale-green shirt that made his eyes glow. His dark hair was smoothed down, and his jeans were slim and snug. In his left hand was a small black bag.

"Mornin', Ava," he said to me with a crooked grin, and I returned the greeting.

Our group moved onto the palace grounds, and we got our tickets and headed inside. The breath locked in my lungs when I stepped into the massive building. Unbelievable.

"This palace is the queen's official Scottish residence," Graham told me as he stepped to my side. Suddenly my body became hyperaware of his every move—the casual strides of his long legs, the way his attention landed with deliberation on each portrait he passed.

Our parents moved from room to room in the State Apartments, and we followed a few feet behind. I couldn't stop staring at the decor. Intricate woodwork was everywhere; even the ceilings were crafted with care. So much craftsmanship.

When we went into the dining room, Graham touched my hand. My skin warmed instantly from the contact.

"Erm." He cleared his throat. "I, uh, brought ya somethin'." He handed me the small black bag.

My heart slammed against my rib cage as I opened it and peered inside. I pulled out a sleek flash drive with the word MUSIC written in Sharpie across its smooth white surface. "Cool, what is this?"

"It's my band. Thought ya might fancy a listen."

I blinked in surprise. "Oh wow. Seriously? I can't wait!" Part of me wanted to run back to the hotel and pop it in my dad's computer so I could listen right now. He'd made me a mix of his band's music? My cheeks flamed.

"There's somethin' else," he prodded me with a nod toward the bag.

I took out the folded fabric and realized it was a black T-shirt. Stamped on the front was a tartan pattern. On the back was the phrase SCOTLAND PRIDE. "Oh, this is awesome," I said. My throat was tight with appreciation over his thoughtfulness. "Thank you. Seriously."

"'Twas nothin'," he said with a wave of his hand.

But it wasn't nothing. He'd remembered our conversation about his music yesterday and had given me a thoughtful, personalized gift. Not to mention the T-shirt. My heart melted a touch, but I tried to play it cool as we continued walking through the apartments. We went up the steep staircase to view Mary, Queen of Scots's chambers. More incredible woodwork everywhere, along with displays of artifacts.

As we strolled, Graham gave me a brief rundown on the history of the chambers and Queen Mary's turbulent rule. His thorough knowledge about his country's history made me once again embarrassed that I didn't know as much about my own. Sure, I was aware of the major facts and events that shaped US history. But his attention to detail and clear pride in the Scottish fight for freedom and independence rang through as he narrated events to me.

"Your country's past was pretty violent," I remarked in a low murmur during a lull in the conversation.

"Many countries have violent pasts," he retorted. "And ours has a history that goes back quite far."

I conceded his point with a nod and tried to think of something I knew about America that might interest him. "Yeah, our country is definitely not as old as Scotland, but we have events in our past that changed America permanently too. Like the Civil War. It was a huge tragedy that still haunts us." I told him how last year during spring break, our family trip had been to Washington, DC, and we'd done a day visit to Gettysburg. "In the museum, you can see old uniforms with rips and bullet holes. There are rusting guns and swords, old photos of people who fought, even journal entries on display. It was heartbreaking to wander around the exhibits and think how many lives were lost during that three-day battle."

"Yer a history buff too," he said, and I could see the intrigue clearly in his gaze.

It made me happy that I had something comparable to teach him. "In some ways, yeah, but I'm not nearly as knowledgeable as you are." Though after this trip, I was going to change that. Seeing Scotland through Graham's eyes made me want to learn more about the world around me. "If you ever make it to America, you should go to Gettysburg," I said. "The battlegrounds are intense and powerful. Even now, after all this time, you can still feel the presence of the battle there. You'd probably love it."

His gaze skittered away from mine, and we walked in silence for a few moments. Had I said something wrong? I pressed my lips together and scrabbled for something else to talk about.

"Um, what's your favorite place in Scotland?" I finally asked him.

He tilted his head as he thought. "That's a right hard question."

"Fair enough," I said with a laugh. "Sometimes that kind of thing can depend on your mood."

"The Highlands are a bonny sight." I heard the smile in his voice and my heart squeezed at the sound. His passion stirred something in me, made me want to dig deeper and find out everything about him.

"I can't wait to see them soon," I replied as we moved to a row of paintings on the wall.

The rest of the palace was just as stunning. It resonated with historical artifacts, from the paintings to the furniture to the decor, and we talked back and forth about what it was like having a queen versus having a president. When we finished touring the palace, we moved to the grounds and the abbey. The air in the roofless, ruined abbey resonated with solemnity, and I stood in hushed awe as I took in the ancient stonework. The weight of hundreds of years of history lingered in the atmosphere.

As groups of people filtered in and out, no one spoke, like none of us wanted to break the reverent silence.

Our walk back down the Royal Mile was relaxed, and our

parents talked easily about this and that. Graham's hand brushed mine when he moved toward me to avoid a giggling cluster of young girls, and my fingers tingled. I could smell the light scent of his soap as the wind carried it in my direction.

This guy was so getting under my skin. Attractive, smart, witty—what was there not to like? Too bad he lived an ocean away.

We walked to Princes Street Gardens and as a group decided to sit and stretch here for a little bit. The sunshine had gotten even warmer since this morning. Graham took a seat beside me, about twenty feet away from our parents, and we both lay down on the thick grass and stared up at the sky.

"So, ya likin' Scotland so far?" he asked me.

"How could I not? I feel like my brain is exploding from all the things I'm learning."

He chuckled, and the light sound rolled over me, filled this little place in my chest, and lingered there. There was something addictive about hearing him laugh. And something even more addictive about being the one to make him do so.

"I've had fun with ya, Ava," he said, gaze still locked on the sky above us.

"Me too," I admitted. A thrill lit in my heart at the realization that I wasn't the only one feeling this . . . thing between us.

A group of kids ran behind us, screaming with glee as they played tag. Graham tucked his arms behind his head, and out of the corner of my eye I saw the line of arm muscles contract with the movement. I traced the profile of his face with my gaze, let my eyes linger on his eyes, his cheekbones, his lips.

Tomorrow our family was going to tour the city of Stirling. Part of me was excited, of course, but the other part couldn't help but feel down. I reached over and touched the black bag, and my heart stirred again about the gifts. I knew Graham and I couldn't go anywhere relationship-wise, but I wanted to keep being around him. Maybe I could convince Mom and Dad to invite them for dinner tomorrow when we got back from Stirling, or at the end of our trip, when we spent our last night in Edinburgh before leaving Scotland.

A puffy cloud passed overhead, and I made myself stop thinking about the end. This vacation was about living in the now. And right now, there was a handsome boy lying only a foot or so away who was humming a pop song under his breath.

When he hit the chorus and I hummed along, he turned his head and shot me a smile that went right to my heart.

Chapter Five

Monday morning I woke up to a face full of sunshine slitting through the window blinds. I'd stayed up later than usual to listen to Graham's music. The songs were really good—his band had talent, and the drums were dead on. When the flash drive had finished playing I'd listened to the whole thing again, which meant I was a bit tired this morning . . . but it was worth it.

I tiptoed over and peeked through the slats to the morning bustle of downtown Edinburgh. It was another bright, sunny day, and the sky was that perfect shade of blue that made you excited to go outside.

Mom was still asleep, but Dad wasn't around—probably downstairs grabbing coffee. He was planning to do one last day of ancestry research in Edinburgh. I took a quick shower and dressed, then came out of the bathroom to find Mom holding her head in her hands.

"You okay?" I asked her.

She gave a soft groan. "My head is killing me."

I frowned. Mom's migraines were rare, but they did happen on occasion. And when they did, she usually spent a full day hiding in her room in complete darkness. I got up and closed the blinds. "Do you have any pain medicine with you?"

"Already took some." She slid deeper into the blankets and sighed, shutting her eyes. "My skull feels like it's been run over by a truck."

"Well, you definitely should stay here and rest up." I bit back a sigh. It was selfish of me to be upset at my plans being changed, and my stomach twinged with guilt. She couldn't help it.

Mom peeked an eye open and looked at me. "I'm sorry, hon. I know you're excited to see Stirling. Maybe give me a couple of hours and we'll see how I'm feeling, okay?"

Our plan was to visit Stirling Castle today and learn about William Wallace, one of the most honored men in Scottish history, remembered for his courage in standing up to England. We'd been looking forward to this day for a while, since we both knew how important he was. But I knew even if she did get out of bed, she'd be miserable and in pain.

"It's okay," I said as I got up and wet a washcloth. I placed it on her forehead. "I can find something to keep me busy around here today."

"I have an idea." Mom grabbed her phone and gingerly punched in numbers. A pause, then in a low tone she said, "Hey! It's Erica. I have a favor to ask. My head is killing me, and I'm pretty sure it's a migraine. Are you busy today? Could I bribe you by buying lunch if you'll take Ava to Stirling Castle?" Pause. "Oh, that's okay—" Another pause, for a minute or so, and then she gave a small sigh of satisfaction. "That sounds perfect. Thank you so much." She hung up and shot me a weak smile.

"What's going on?" I asked her.

"I called Mollie to ask if she could take you around today, but she has to work and can't get the day off. But Graham is free, and he said he'd be happy to escort you. He'll be here in about twenty minutes."

"Oh, I see." I tried to ignore the excited flutter in my stomach and aimed for a casual tone. "Well, that'll be fun. Thanks for arranging that."

Dad walked into the room and pressed a small kiss to the top of Mom's head. "How are you feeling?"

She tried to smile at him, but it wobbled a bit, and my heart squeezed in sympathy. "I'm okay. I'm just gonna sleep in here for a while, and Ava's going out with Graham to Stirling for the day. He and his dad are on their way to pick her up."

"Mom, are you sure this is okay? Why don't I just stay here with you? I really appreciate you setting this up for me, but I don't want to leave you alone in pain." Of course I'd love to hang out with Graham, to have another day to get to know him more, but I didn't like seeing her suffer and wanted to help somehow. "I'll be quiet, and I can fetch things for you."

She reached over and squeezed my hand, and her eyes shone with gratitude. "It's okay, I promise. I'm just going to sleep. No sense in you staying here bored. You have your phone, right? I'll send you a message when I wake up. Not to mention your father will be local, so I can always call him if I need something." She grimaced and touched her head with her free hand. "Now both of you, get out of here. Go have fun today, please. It will help me feel better."

"I'm coming back at noon to check on you," Dad said firmly. He got a glass of water and left it on her bedside. He dropped a kiss on her lips and stroked her hair.

She nodded and closed her eyes. "Thanks, Paul."

I adjusted the wet washcloth and stood, and Dad and I exited the hotel room, me with my camera bag draped across my chest. It would be the perfect day for gorgeous shots of Scotland, though my heart fluttered just a bit in nervous anticipation of seeing Graham again.

Dad wrapped an arm around my shoulders and squeezed me to his side. "She'll be okay, pumpkin. I'm nearby. The sleep will do her good."

"Yeah, I know you're right." And she would definitely call us if she needed anything.

Dad peered down at me. "So. You're spending more time with this boy, huh?"

My face flamed. "It's very nice of him to offer to tour me around."

"Uh-huh."

"He's quite knowledgeable about Scotland's history, you know."

"Yeah."

"In fact, I bet today is going to be like a school lesson."

"Where the teacher is your age and happens to be super attractive."

Busted. I tried not to grin. "It's not my fault that the youth of today are smarter than ever."

His lips quirked. "*Behave,* princess. And you'd better check in with me frequently. I want hourly text messages."

I saluted him, and he rolled his eyes.

Dad waited with me on the side of the street until a pristine white van showed up. When he saw Steaphan wave, he gave a hearty wave back. "Okay, have fun. And don't forget to check in."

I pressed a kiss to his cheek. "Go learn more about our heritage. I can't wait to hear what you find today."

My hands trembled as I reached for the van door, but it flew open before I could touch the handle. Graham's smile lit me from the inside, and I couldn't help my own responding smile.

"Mornin'," he said as he waved me in.

"Thank you so much—," I started, then stopped when I got inside and saw a guy and a girl sitting in the back row. "Oh. Hi."

The guy, who had dark-brown hair and a handsome face,

grinned at me with bright white teeth. "Good mornin'! I'm Jamison. Graham told us yer visitin' Stirling, and we wanted to come. Hope that's all right. This here's my sister, Kylie."

His sister, who looked just like him but with delicate features, eyed me with bold curiosity. She nodded her greeting, then turned her focus to Graham, who was settling into the second row.

"Come on in," Steaphan said in a booming voice. "Let's get goin'."

I took the empty seat beside Graham and tried not to think about the length of his thigh pressed against mine. I turned around to face the siblings and hoped my smile didn't give away my surprise. "I'm Ava. Really happy to meet you guys!"

Steaphan drove off, and the van hummed its way down the road. I peered out the window to watch the buildings and rolling green fields fly by. Why had Graham asked his friends to come along? Did he not want to be alone with me? Had I been misreading yesterday's interactions?

I shook off this train of thought. He was taking time out of his day to play tour guide with me. The least I could do was be kind and thoughtful. No, I hadn't made up our moments yesterday, and his friends coming along with us didn't mean he didn't want to be with me. In fact, maybe he felt like we were starting to connect and he was comfortable introducing me to his friends.

The thought buoyed my spirits. "I'm super excited to see the castle," I said in a low tone. "Thank you guys for coming along. It's going to be a blast."

"Sorry to hear yer ma is ill," Graham said. Empathy poured from his eyes.

"Thanks," I replied. "By the way, I listened to your songs."

There was a slight flutter at the base of his throat. "And?"

"They were awesome. You guys are so talented! I wish I could see you play live, because I bet it's even better."

His face flashed gratitude, and he moved a fraction closer to me on the seat. "Thanks."

Jamison leaned forward to duck his head between us. "So, this is yer first visit to Scotland, aye? How are ya likin' it?"

"It's wonderful," I replied in a rushed breath.

We spent the rest of the ride to Stirling talking about Edinburgh and the sights I'd seen so far. Kylie was quiet for the most part, but I noticed how often her gaze drifted to Graham. It was so obvious she liked him that I couldn't believe he didn't seem to realize it too.

"We're here!" Steaphan said as he pulled up to a large gravel parking lot. "I'll be back this afternoon to pick ya up. Behave," he said with a mock stare at the guys.

"I'll make sure they do," Kylie said as she rested her hands on her brother's and Graham's shoulders.

Jealousy pinched in my chest, but I made myself keep my chin up as I exited the van. "Thank you for the ride," I told Graham's dad.

We made our way to the castle, and I gasped as I stared up at the massive stone facade, wrapped in a stone wall and sitting on top of a large crag. Powerful, dominating, the castle walls were huge and attention-grabbing.

As we walked through the entrance, Graham stood to my right and filled me in on William Wallace and another man named Robert the Bruce, who was also important in Scottish history in its battle for independence from England. I'd done a little studying up on this, so I was prepared for a real interaction this time and brought up what I'd researched online about Wallace.

We all went to the palace first, and I blinked at the opulence around me. Rich tapestries, lush velvet furniture—it was gorgeous.

"I don't know as much about Stirling as I do about Edinburgh," Graham admitted. "But everyone knows about the great battle that took place here."

I nodded as I tried not to stare into those bright-blue eyes. They seemed to sparkle a bit extra today and drew me in. "Yeah. I read about that, too. It was—"

"Graham!" Kylie slipped up to his side and threaded her arm through his. "Jamison and I were just talkin'. Remember our primary school trip here?"

A hearty laugh erupted from him, and he nodded at her. "That wee boy who ripped off his keks and ran across the field in nothin' but his underwear?"

I giggled at the mental image. That had to be hilarious. "Wow, none of my elementary school field trips went like that. The worst we had was a kid who kept swallowing pennies he found on the ground." We'd visited downtown Cleveland that day. The trip had ended with him being rushed to the emergency room. He'd come to school the next day all sullen and pasty-looking.

Kylie blinked her long eyelashes at Graham and whispered in his ear, and his grin grew wider. I thinned my lips and tried to fight down the sudden flare-up of jealousy. It was painfully obvious the girl was sending me heavy signs. She liked Graham and wanted me to know.

Message received, Kylie.

Well, I wasn't about to pick a fight over her actions. I moved to Jamison's side and struck up a conversation with him, and the four of us drifted upstairs to check out the gallery of Stirling heads, a bunch of carved wooden portraits.

"That man's beard is amazing," I joked to Jamison, pointing toward one portrait. I took a picture of it.

His face fell. "That's me ancestor, Ava."

"Oh, I'm sorry—"

"Nah, just teasin' ya," he said with a wide smirk.

I wrinkled my nose and shoved his shoulder. "You had me going there for a moment. I was afraid I'd offended you." I eyed the rest of the room and saw Graham standing several feet away beside Kylie. She was talking in an animated fashion with him, but his eyes were locked on me.

I swallowed as a flush stole across my cheeks.

When Kylie finished talking, he strode over to us, and my heart stuttered. His face looked intense, his gaze locked on mine. "Ready to explore the rest of the castle grounds, Ava?" he asked.

There was a hint of something in his voice I couldn't quite identify. But it pulled at me.

"Definitely," I said, aware I sounded a bit breathy.

Kylie came up behind us and rested her slender fingers on Graham's shoulder, but he didn't turn around to face her this time. He peered at me for another long moment, and then with a smile he waved us toward the stairs leading out of the palace.

The rest of the day flew by. An unspoken, multilayered message had passed between the two of us in the Stirling head gallery, one that made me hyperaware of him. He remained pretty close to my side, cupping my elbow to guide me into rooms, resting his hand on my lower back as he leaned in close to talk about exhibits. By the time his dad arrived to load us into the van and take us back to Edinburgh, I was almost on sensory overload.

Graham had completely taken over my mind and senses.

Kylie declared from the backseat, "We should go to Glasgow tomorrow."

"Oh, aye!" Jamison said in hearty enthusiasm. "I have no plans. Graham? Ava?"

"I'm supposed to go to St. Andrews with my parents," I said with a sigh. "They want to golf."

We hit a bump, and Graham's knee pressed into mine, which set off a round of tingles in my leg.

"Do *you* golf?" he asked me.

I shook my head and laughed. "Dad tried to teach me, but it

went horribly. I think I hit the ball once, and it went twenty feet off to the side."

His eyes flashed as he leaned toward me, and his warm breath caressed the hairs on the side of my face. "Let's ask yer folks if ya can come with us instead. It'll be fun."

"Aye, what do ya say, Ava?" Jamison asked as he clapped me on the shoulder.

I peered back at Kylie but couldn't read her face. Well, she was the one who'd suggested it in the first place. Maybe she didn't view me as a threat to her relationship with Graham. A small, stubborn part of me actually wanted to be a threat. Wanted Graham to see me not just as a vacation girl but as something that could be more.

Because every moment I spent in his presence made me want that too.

"Let's do it," I said with a resolute nod. "It'll be fun."

Chapter ● Six

This. Is. Amazing." I snapped a photograph of Doulton Fountain, an ornate brick fountain in Glasgow Green that spurted water from several spots around its circumference. We'd been dropped off by Graham's dad at the Glasgow park about an hour ago and had spent the morning so far wandering around, soaking in the sunshine of another beautiful day. We'd been blessed by the weather gods so far on this trip.

Jamison nodded toward a brick building off to the left of the fountain. "Over there's Templeton's Carpet Factory."

I chuckled as I shook my head. Even the carpet factory looked luxurious and important.

Glasgow was nothing like I'd imagined. Art and commerce thrived in this city, which intrigued me with its old and new elements mashed together. One sterling example was the People's Palace, nestled right behind the fountain, with its old brick facade mingled with a glass dome structure. Crazy and fun. Corinne, a classical artist at heart, would probably hate the glass addition. I kind of liked it.

"Ready to go in yet?" Graham asked me with a wave toward the People's Palace.

I nodded, and Kylie and Jamison stepped behind the two of us as we made our way in. I still couldn't believe my parents had let me come, but I'd begged them not to make me watch them golf. They'd laughingly agreed, so long as I checked in regularly. I think part of them wanted to have a romantic day to themselves, something I was all too happy to provide.

After all, it meant another day with Graham.

Plus, it didn't hurt that Graham's dad was going to be in Glasgow all day and would check in with us this afternoon. So we weren't stranded here alone without a parent nearby.

Kylie slipped between me and Graham and shot him a flashy smile. She had on tight jeans and a black shirt that flattered her curves. She really was a lovely girl; several guys had shot appreciative glances her way since we'd arrived at the park. Not that she'd noticed them. She only had eyes for Graham. "We'll go to a chippy after this, aye?" she asked him as she blinked those long lashes his way.

He peered over her head to look at me. "You in?"

"What's a chippy?" I asked.

Jamison laughed, and Kylie tittered. "A fish-and-chips shop," Jamison said with a wide grin.

"Oh. Yeah." I should have guessed that—Mom had mentioned before that in Great Britain, they called french fries "chips." My face flushed a bit, and I gave a stiff nod. "Sounds good."

I kept my focus ahead as we entered the museum. To my delight, the glass enclosure contained a lush garden. Graham, Jamison, and Kylie were talking about which chippy they wanted to go to, so I slipped away and strolled around the U-shape, snapping pictures of the well-groomed plants.

"Ava!" Graham called out.

I turned and took a photograph of the three of them, standing casual and familiar together.

Kylie stepped closer to Graham and wrapped her arms around both guys. "Wait, I wasn't ready!" she said with a mock pout. "Can ya take another?"

I did, and then took a couple zoomed in on Graham's face. It hadn't escaped my attention that today was my last day with him. The fact that I'd even had these two bonus days was a gift, and I intended to make the most of it.

And that included not being bugged by my jealousy of Kylie. Well, as much as humanly possible, anyway.

I popped the lens on my camera and said, "Let's go inside."

The museum was eclectic, packed with displays set up to show what Glasgow homes looked like in earlier times. We wandered with the flow of the crowd for an hour or so, moving from exhibit to exhibit. When a woman holding a baby tried to shove her way through our group, Graham took my hand to pull me out of the way. It was so hard to let it go.

After we left the museum, we found a chippy. Our meals were wrapped in newspaper, which was a bit odd, but the fish was to die for. I devoured it and the chips, which made Jamison laugh.

"I have a hearty appetite," I said with a laugh. "And I'm not ashamed."

"Every lad likes a lass who enjoys food," Jamison replied.

I had to admit, the guy was really attractive. Something about the open friendliness on his face drew me to him and encouraged my own responding smiles. He made me laugh a lot, and I found him fresh and entertaining. But Jamison didn't make my skin tingle, didn't impact me the way Graham did.

I liked him, but it wasn't *that* kind of like.

"Where to now?" Kylie asked as she dabbed the corners of her mouth. Every move of hers was delicate and feminine.

"Can we find an art museum?" I asked them. "Or I'd love to check out a gallery."

"Wait, I know where we can go," Graham said with a smile. He eyed me. "You'll like it, I'm sure."

We tossed our trash and walked until we made it to the front of a large stone building with Grecian-like columns. The small set of steps leading to the entrance beckoned me.

"The Gallery of Modern Art," I read on a sign, and clapped with glee. I turned to him. "That's perfect! I love modern art."

Kylie sighed. "Can we go shopping instead? I'm a bit muse-umed out."

Jamison shoved against her side and shot her a warning glare.

I swallowed down my flare of irritation and gave her a smile that I hoped looked sincere. "I'd be happy to go shopping after we finish looking around here. Or if you want to go ahead, I can meet you when I'm done." Because there was no way I was leaving without taking a peek in here.

Her gaze darted to Graham, then back to me. "No, no, I'll go with ya."

As we walked inside, Jamison said from behind us in a smooth voice, "Did ya know this building used to be the mansion of a tobacco lord? Since then it's also been a bank, a library, and now it's a museum."

I blinked and turned to face him. "How did you know all that?"

He held up his phone, opened to a browser page, and shot me a wink. "The World Wide Web," he declared.

With a laugh, I shook my head. "I should have thought of doing that. Good idea."

We made our way inside and moved through the exhibits. When we saw one that was a precarious pile of colored chairs and purses, sitting in the middle of a black-and-white tiled floor, we stopped in unison.

Kylie tilted her head. "What does that mean?"

"I have no idea," I murmured.

"I'm not sure it even matters what it means," Graham said in an offhanded tone.

Kylie shot him a strange look and moved toward the cluster of chairs.

As she and her brother circled the exhibit, I turned to him. "Why do you think it doesn't matter?" I asked in a quiet tone.

He pursed his lips, deep in thought. The bold dark-green shade of his long-sleeved shirt made his eyes pop, and I could smell that fresh-soap scent coming off him. I took a step closer and let myself breathe him in.

"Art is so personal, so intimate," he said on a soft exhale, and I swallowed in reaction to the soft cadence of his words. "Meanin' can vary by person—even vary by day, depending on yer mood."

"That's true. I guess there's no sense in trying to label something when each person is going to give the work of art their own label." I crooked a smile his way. "Are you into art?"

"Me? Nah." A dimple popped out in his left cheek. "But music is similar. I love songs that take risks, that challenge us."

My chest warmed, and I nodded. "Me too. I love it when art makes you think. When it isn't safe or predictable and can't fit in a neat little box. My friend Corinne, she's in an art workshop this summer with an amazing African artist. I'd been tempted to sign up for it, but I decided not to. Now I'm glad I didn't." A slow burn crawled across my face when I realized what I'd said.

"Why are ya glad?" His eyes seemed to bore into mine, and the soft noises around us faded away.

I swallowed as my stomach gave a nervous lurch. Did I dare tell him the truth? What did I have to lose, really? "Because if I had taken the workshop, I wouldn't be here in Scotland walking around with you." My pulse pounded hard in my ears, and I felt a slight tremble in my hands.

Graham took a step toward me, numerous emotions flickering through his eyes. We were so close I could practically feel the crackle in the air between us. "I'm glad yer here, Ava. I said it before—I've had a lot of fun getting to know ya."

"Me too." I bit my lower lip. Graham was full of layers, an intriguing puzzle, and I wanted to pick his brain more.

His eyes darted down to my mouth, then jumped back up again, and I saw his jaw clench for a moment. What was he thinking about? Kissing me? I'd give anything to know what was going on in his head right now.

My phone buzzed, and I gave an awkward laugh as I dug it out of my pocket.

Hey, honey! Having fun? Where are you guys? :-)

"A text from my mom," I said to him. "She probably wants to make sure I'm still alive." I took a picture of the chair and purse exhibit and sent it to her, along with a brief description of what we'd seen in Glasgow so far.

"Graham?" Kylie said from behind us. "Check out these paintings over here. They're just stripes and patterns."

I followed behind and watched him and Kylie talk. His body language with her was different than it was with me. Was that bad? Or was it a good thing? I kept getting these vibes from him that made me think he wasn't only interested in being my friend.

The last thing I wanted to do, though, was read a message that wasn't there—or make it have more meaning than it actually did. Being burned so badly with David had made me cautious.

Jamison grabbed my elbow and, with a smirk, nudged me up behind Graham and Kylie. We stared at the two large paintings mounted on the half wall in front of a row of columns.

"Seriously," Kylie declared, "I don't get how this is art. It's just patterns."

"To some people, patterns are art," I replied. "There's beauty in the repetition."

She shrugged. "I guess." It was obvious by the look on her face that she wasn't trying to be rude or insulting. She genuinely didn't understand.

"My friend back home is the same as you," I offered. "She prefers classical art and paintings to modern works. I don't think there's anything wrong with having particular art tastes, for what it's worth, so long as you have respect for other art. It doesn't mean you have to like everything. I think good art challenges us to think outside our regular world and view things differently."

Her eyes flicked to me, and she gave me a brief but warm nod. Her demeanor relaxed a bit when she apparently realized I wasn't going to insult her. "Yeah, that's a fair point. Thanks."

We continued walking through the gallery, and as Jamison took Kylie over to a brightly painted canvas on a creamy beige wall, Graham stepped to my side.

"That was nice of ya," he said. His hand brushed my lower back for the briefest of seconds.

My pulse fluttered. "Oh, uh, thanks."

"She's a kind lass if ya get to know her," he offered.

"How long have you all known each other?"

He and I strolled around the perimeter of this room, pausing before each painting. They consisted of thick slashes and blobs of rich-colored paint splashed across large canvases.

"A long time. Since I was a young lad. We live in the same neighborhood." The fondness ringing clear in his voice and eyes made my heart sink a touch, and I instantly chastised myself for the reaction.

Graham's arm brushed mine. He leaned down and whispered in my ear, "I'm startin' to think she has a wee crush on me."

I bit back a barking laugh. A "wee crush" to say the least. "Yeah, I think you're right about that."

As he pulled back to look at me, his lips twitched. "It's obvious to you, eh?"

Like I could blame the girl for how she felt. I had a crush on him too. I couldn't hide from my feelings anymore, even if they'd happened crazy fast. I'd known this guy for a few days, but already he'd started working his way under my skin with his charm and wit and intelligence.

I stared down at my feet, unsure what to reply and suddenly feeling like my emotions were on display for him, for everyone in the gallery to read. If I could sense Kylie's crush, surely others could sense mine.

He nudged me with his shoulder, and I looked up. "She and I are just friends, yanno," he said quietly. "It's not like that."

My heart jumped to my throat. I nodded in response, though the gesture was wooden. They might only be friends now, but that didn't mean it would always be that way. "Do you, uh, have a girl-friend?" I asked him.

He shook his head. "Do ya have a boyfriend?"

I shook my head, and we both gave awkward chuckles.

"Kinda surprised ya don't," he said, and I could hear the earnestness in his tone. "Yer a bonny gal."

Oh wow. I bit my lower lip and felt my cheeks start to burn. I shrugged. "Just been waiting for the right person."

His eyes seemed to pierce right into me. "Me too, Ava."

Chapter ● Seven

The soft late-afternoon breezes swept through the streets as we made our way to the park after wandering in and out of quaint local shops. Jamison had heard there was a dance troupe performing at the park tonight. We'd checked in with Steaphan first to let him know our plans, and he said he'd pick us up at nine to take us home.

Something had changed in our group dynamic in the art museum. As we'd wandered through the exhibits, Kylie had begun to relax and stopped being so uptight, and as a result, more of her natural attitude began to shine through. We'd giggled over some of the stranger exhibits on display, wondering what the artist's inspiration was. She'd even bought me a bottle of water when I'd mentioned I was thirsty.

It made me feel even guiltier about liking Graham as much as I did. The longing gazes she threw his way when he wasn't looking were almost painful to see, especially now that I was starting to enjoy her company.

"What's Ohio look like?" Jamison asked me.

Our group approached the east end of the park, and as we walked, I described Ohio's eclectic scenery—the tree-covered hills, the flat farmlands with rows of corn that stretched as far as the eye could see, the bustling big cities and quaint small towns.

"It's awesome. I've lived in the Cleveland area my whole life, and I can't imagine living anywhere else," I explained with a smile. "There's little that can beat Ohio in the fall, when all the leaves are brilliant colors on the trees. I wish I had a picture on my phone to show you."

"Sounds quite bonny," Kylie said. "The Highlands are unlike anything ya've ever seen too."

"I can't wait. The photographs are so beautiful, and the real thing has to be even better." I sipped my water, and we found a place under a shade tree to sit and wait for the dance troupe's performance in a half hour.

Though it was already late afternoon, the sun was surprisingly warm, and I stripped off my jacket and tucked it under myself to sit on. Graham was on my right, Jamison on my left, and Kylie beside Graham.

We talked about everything and nothing as we waited. I learned that Jamison was an excellent long-distance runner with aspirations to try out for the Olympics someday. He and Kylie had an easygoing relationship, interrupting each other and poking fun, but none of the antagonism you sometimes saw with siblings.

While we talked, Graham was quiet, just watching us all, only chiming in here or there. He seemed content to sit back and let us chatter.

"I'm dying of thirst," Kylie proclaimed. She jumped up and dusted off her backside. "Anyone else fancy a drink?"

"I'm quite thirsty myself," Jamison said and stood as well. "We'll go find sustenance and be back."

"Graham, care for anything?" she asked him.

"Nah, I'm good, thanks." He gave her a polite smile.

The two of them walked off, with Kylie shooting him a quick look over her shoulder before they crossed the street toward a shop.

A comfortable silence settled between the two of us. I stretched my hands out along the grass, and my fingers brushed against his. With an awkward laugh, I jerked away and tucked my hands in my lap.

"So, what else do ya do in yer free time?" he asked me. "Other than art and traveling to beautiful countries, that is."

I kept my gaze on my sneakered feet so I wouldn't stare into his eyes. "Well, I like to swim laps. I practically live in our neighborhood's outdoor pool during the summer. I've learned how to knit, and I've started making the world's longest scarf. And I go to our school's meditation club—"

I heard a low chuckle and stopped talking to look at him. His right eyebrow was straight up in the air. "Meditation club?"

"Yeah, it's to help us relax after being all stressed out after a rough day at school." I grinned. "We drink tea, talk for a little bit, then sit in silence and release our worries into the atmosphere." Sometimes I was even able to convince Corinne to join me, though she was usually too busy doing homework.

"Sounds lovely." His lips quirked, and a dimple appeared in his left cheek. "We don't have anything like that at my school. What do you worry about that requires you to meditate?"

"My grades, especially English and math. Those are my weak spots. Not to mention trying to figure out what colleges I want to start checking out, and when I should look for a job . . ." I shook off the familiar knot of tension that started to build in my stomach and nudged him with my shoulder. "And what do *you* do for fun? Other than drumming and dancing around the Highlands in a kilt, that is," I teased.

In the middle of the grass in front of us, a few members of the dance troupe arrived, clad in green-plaid kilts, dark-green vests, and kneesocks.

Graham looked them over, then turned his attention back to me. "Well, I work with my da sometimes on repairin' cars. He has an old hot rod we've been fixin' for a coupla years now."

"That's cool. Do you think you'll get to drive it when it's fixed?"

He paused, and his back stiffened for a second or two, and an expression flitted across his face that I couldn't quite name.

"Probably not," he finally said to me. "Look, Jamison and Kylie are back."

Okay, apparently Graham didn't want to talk any more about this. Why would the car be such a big deal to him? Was he not eager to drive, or was there something else at play here?

My heart fluttered, and I forced a broad smile as the siblings took their seats once again.

"The dancers are warming up," Jamison said to me in a low whisper. He dug into his pocket and pulled out a small red package. "I brought ya somethin'."

I peered down at the wrapper and read the text. "Butter shortbread rounds. Are these cookies?" My stomach gave a low grumble in anticipation.

"These're *only* the best biscuits around." His grin was wide. "Give 'em a try."

I opened the bag and breathed in the rich scent, then took two out and handed him one. We both bit into them at the same time, and I groaned at the delicious buttery-sweet goodness. "Oh wow, you weren't kidding. This is the best cookie I've had in forever."

"What are you two going on about?" Graham said from beside me.

I turned and thrust the bag toward him. "Would you and Kylie like a cookie? Uh, a biscuit? Jamison bought them for me. They're so good."

A look passed between the two guys. If I didn't know better, I'd think Graham was a touch jealous. His lips were a bit thin, his smile a little too wide to seem genuine. "I've had 'em before," he said.

Kylie had no qualms and snagged a cookie from the bag. "Thanks!"

Musicians began to arrive: a guy lugging a bagpipe wearing a kilt, a drummer, and a woman standing with them. She started some vocal exercises, and they warmed up their instruments.

Jamison, Kylie, and I finished the cookies, and I got up and tossed the bag away in a nearby garbage can. When I returned to our tree, I noticed the two guys' heads tucked together as they talked in quiet whispers. I slowed my pace during my approach; they pulled apart when they saw me, and Jamison wore a face-splitting smirk. Graham wouldn't meet my eyes.

My stomach clenched. What had happened? I'd obviously missed something. Too bad I wasn't good friends with Kylie, or else I'd ask her what they'd talked about while I was gone. But I didn't want to rock the boat and bring up my curiosity over Graham. Not when we were starting to get along so well.

I plopped down between them and tried to pretend like I didn't care what was happening. It was obvious they'd been talking about me, but neither was going to act like it. Okay then. I stretched my legs out in front of me and smiled, watching the dancers warm up, the singer do her mouth exercises. I was totally not going to pay any attention to how close Graham was, or why he didn't seem to want to look at me now.

It didn't matter in the least.

The embarrassed sting in my heart told me otherwise.

The dancers started, and people clapped as they stomped and

ᆫᄒ-ᆫᅡᆫᆫᆫ

kicked and whirled. After a while, I found myself getting caught up in the beauty of their movements. The music was simple but heartfelt, and the girls were pouring their emotions and energy into their dance. I wanted to learn how to do it—maybe when I got home I could find a place giving lessons.

"Gorgeous, isn't it?" Graham whispered right in my ear.

The caress of his breath on my skin made me shiver, but I kept my composure and didn't give my reaction away. "Very." It was evident how hard they practiced; they were perfectly in sync with one another as they whirled around and changed positions.

I grabbed my camera from my bag and snapped a few action shots. With the setting sun glinting in the dancers' hair, making their skin glow, the pictures came out better than I'd hoped they would.

As the crowd clapped to the rhythm, we joined in, and soon the whole area surrounding the dancers was filled with clapping and cheering. I whistled loudly.

All too soon they stopped, and the park roared with applause and cheers. The dancers were flushed and sweating, their hair plastered to their brows, but the lightness in their eyes and their wide smiles showed their pleasure. I took a few more shots and then some of the crowd.

Graham grabbed his phone and checked the time. "My da will pick us up in a half hour." His voice sounded a little flat, and as I put my camera away, I struggled to find the right words to ask him what was going on. I didn't want to pry, but it was obvious he wasn't his usual self.

Kylie bounded out of her seat and ran over to talk to the dancers, and Jamison took off with her. I saw him smooth a hand over his dark hair and straighten his posture, and I bit back a chuckle. The guy was a total flirt.

"You okay?" I finally asked Graham. "You seem a bit . . . off. Or maybe it's just me. After all, it's not like I know you that well or anything, and I could be wrong." *Oh God, someone make me stop blabbing on.* I bit my lower lip and looked away.

He sighed. "It's not just you. Sorry. Lot on my mind this evenin'."

"Anything I can help with?" I turned to face him.

He stared at me for a long moment, and that crackle of tension lit between us. "Not really, but I appreciate ya askin'. Quite kind of ya." The smile he gave me this time was genuine, and he leaned a bit closer to me. "Have a good time today?"

"A great time," I gushed. "It's been awesome. Actually, everything has been fun so far. Edinburgh, Stirling, Glasgow . . . I can't wait for what's next." And yet, the next phase of our vacation, starting tomorrow, took me away from Graham for the remainder of my trip. My throat tightened with unexpected emotion.

Graham's brow knitted as he studied my face. "Hmm, ya don't seem so thrilled, though."

How honest should I be right now? Should I tell him the truth—that I couldn't get him off my mind? He'd probably think

I was insane. After all, I was a vacationing tourist. He was a gorgeous local boy. There wasn't anywhere we could go from here.

And yet . . . I wanted it to, because he made me feel a way I'd never felt before. This wasn't just a shallow crush. Graham had depths I wanted to explore, and he made me think, made me laugh. Maybe he'd write to me when I got home, and we could start from there. Even just as friends. Relationships started with friendship all the time. And with the Internet, the world was smaller than ever.

I swallowed past the tightness in my throat and admitted, "I am thrilled for the most part. But I've had a lot of fun with you, and we're leaving on our bus tour tomorrow. So . . ." My face burned hot, and it was hard to keep looking into those intense eyes. I cleared my throat. "Um, I don't know, I was hoping maybe we could keep talking somehow, because I've really enjoyed our conversations."

The tension in his body relaxed in an instant, and the smile he shot me was so charming the air locked in my lungs. Graham gave a soft, warm laugh, and that dimple popped out again. His teeth flashed in the setting sun. "I don't think that's going to be a problem, Ava."

I blinked in surprise. "Okay . . . ?"

"My da's running yer bus tour," he explained, and his grin grew wider. "I'll be accompanyin' ya through the Highlands, ya see."

"Oh," I breathed, and a warm flush settled over my skin.

"We'll be seeing a lot more of each other." His eyes danced in amusement. "I hope that's okay."

Okay? It was more than okay. It was the best thing I could have hoped for. On the inside, I was jumping up and down. But I kept my cool for the most part, even though I couldn't fight the grin on my face. "It'll be fun."

Another week with Graham? It felt like a birthday present. The chance to delve into Scotland's most epic locales with the guy I was crushing on. Not to mention the look in his eyes, the way he was leaning toward me, giving me heavy hints this crush wasn't one-sided. It was real, and with more time to develop, who knew what could happen?

Kylie and Jamison returned, and our group conversation went back to its normal light filler as we walked to our pickup spot. But there was a buoyancy in my chest now, and I knew I was grinning like an idiot. Luckily, no one commented on it.

"Okay, everyone," I proclaimed a few minutes before Steaphan was supposed to get us. "The three of you gather together so I can get another couple of shots."

With my phone, I took a full-body pic, then zoomed in on all their faces and snapped another shot. After that, I got the siblings' contact information and saved it so we could keep in touch.

Steaphan arrived and waved at us.

Kylie and I hugged. "Thanks for touring around with me," I told her.

"It was a blast," she said, and her smile was genuine. She opened the side door and hopped in.

Jamison leaned in to give me a hug. "He likes ya," he whispered in my ear.

I stiffened in shock; my heart thudded painfully in my chest. It was one thing to feel it—quite another to hear someone else say it. Could this be what they were discussing earlier?

"Just thought ya should know. Don't tell him I told. He'd kill me." He pulled away from our embrace and winked, then sauntered off into the back row.

Graham, unaware of what had just passed between me and Jamison, hopped inside, and I followed him. The whole ride back to Edinburgh, we bounced along the way, our knees and thighs brushing. And all I could hear was Jamison's voice, telling me Graham liked me.

He *liked* me.

Chapter ● Eight

had to admit, I was kind of sad to pack up my belongings and leave this hotel room. It had been my Edinburgh home for the last few days. But we were on to the next portion of our trip—our weeklong travel through the Highlands. I could hardly wait.

I folded my clothes and tucked them back into my two suit-cases. When that was done, I put my camera bag and sketching materials in my backpack, so I could have them handy for our photo-op stops. Then I sat on the edge of the bed and watched as Mom and Dad finished gathering their stuff. Steaphan had told Dad he'd pick us up in half an hour. Naturally, my stomach had been one big knot of excitement since I'd gotten up this morning.

"I'm going to miss Edinburgh," Mom said with a sigh as she

walked over and peered out the hotel window. "I can't believe how this place has grown on me, even in a short period of time."

"I was just thinking that too," I said.

"Still, I'm sure sightseeing in the Highlands will be unbelievable," Mom said as she turned around and leaned back against the windowpane. Her brow quirked. "Not to mention the 'local attractions.'"

I squinted at her. Subtlety wasn't one of her stronger traits. "Very funny." She was right, though. It had taken me forever to fall asleep last night, since I was eager to spend more time with Graham. This thing between us was a heady rush I didn't want to shake off. Plus, I couldn't stop thinking about Jamison's words to me.

A bus tour with him through one of the most romantic places ever would be a memory of a lifetime.

Dad went to unplug his computer, and I jumped up. "Wait!" I said as I plopped into the desk chair. "Can I please send Corinne a message?"

It was only a little after three a.m. back in Cleveland, since they were five hours behind us, so she wouldn't get it for a while, but I wanted to at least say hi. I hadn't written to her much after my first day or so around Scotland, and I wasn't sure what cell phone or Internet reception would be like where we were going. Somehow I didn't imagine the Highlands were covered with an extensive network of cell phone towers.

He nodded. "Okay, but make it quick, princess. We need to be in the lobby in fifteen minutes."

I gave him a grateful smile, then logged on to the chat messenger.

> **AvaBee: Hey! I know you're snoozing right now. Are U having sweet dreams about a certain hunky guy we both know? ;-)**

Before I'd left for Scotland, Corinne had expressed more than a little frustration at her current situation. She'd been chosen by her art teacher to represent her classroom in a prestigious nation-wide art competition. Only catch was she had to do a joint project with Matthew, a guy she thought was just a jock. But to paraphrase Shakespeare, Corinne was protesting a bit too much. I could tell that Matthew was really getting under her skin. She'd never been this rattled by someone before.

My fingers hovered over the computer keys, and a flash of guilt hit my chest. I hadn't talked to her about Graham yet. I mean, what could I really say? This was just a crazy vacation crush, after all, something she and I would giggle about at our next sleepover as we studied pictures of his face. Even as I thought that, something in my heart throbbed. My past crushes hadn't been this intense this fast. They didn't compare.

Well, I just needed time to figure things out before I talked about it. He and I were still so shy around each other in some ways, and he hadn't come right out and told me he liked me. That hesitation, and the fear of repeating my past mistakes, kept me from telling Corinne about him.

Instead I wrote a little bit describing what I'd seen so far in Scotland, and I promised to send her more pictures once I found an Internet connection.

> **AvaBee: OK, now I have to go. Dad's breathing down my neck, lol. XOXO**

I signed off, logged out, and thanked him.

We gathered our things and left the room. I snapped one last picture of it before Dad closed the door, and we headed to the lobby to wait for Steaphan to pick us up. Mom had said Mollie would be too busy working to come with us on the Highlands tour, so it would be just Steaphan and Graham.

Apparently, there were two other families joining us, one from Germany and one from Sweden. A small group, so the bus wouldn't be filled. Hopefully they were nice people.

Dad walked over to the counter to check us out, then rejoined us a couple of minutes later. "We're good to go, and I confirmed our room reservation for our last day in Scotland," he told Mom. He patted his pocket, which had paper sticking out of it.

Right after that, a short, dark-green bus pulled up in front of the lobby, and Mom clapped in glee. "Yay, he's here!"

We grabbed our luggage and stepped outside. My heart thrummed so wildly I was afraid it would beat its way out of my rib cage. The door on the side of the bus opened, and Steaphan shot us a beaming smile.

"Good mornin'!" he declared as he stepped out and shook Dad's hand, then Mom's. "So excited to have ya onboard. Ready for the trip?"

I nodded, and my gaze drifted toward the bus door when I saw Graham standing there. He hopped out and grabbed our suitcases, while his dad opened the sides of the bus to pop them in.

When he was done, he turned to me, and the breath caught in my throat. His eyes were rich, sparkling this morning, and his slim-fit black T-shirt flattered his lean figure. "Mornin', Ava," he said in a low tone that rumbled across my skin.

Oh man, the look in his gaze held a promise of fun to come. I swallowed my nervousness down and shot him a wobbly grin. That hesitation I'd seen in his eyes before was totally gone right now.

"Morning, Graham," I said, not surprised that my voice conveyed my breathlessness. I slung my backpack over my shoulder and followed him onto the bus.

The interior was cozy, with gray fabric covering the plush seats. In the second row were a family of thin, dark blonds—a man, a woman, and a teenage girl with stunning bright green eyes. She nodded as I entered.

Right behind them was another row of people, two adults with two younger boys who looked around six or so. From listening to the way the mom talked to the boys, it sounded like they were the Germans.

Graham took a seat in the front row, and I made my way to the back, my parents right behind me.

"We all on?" Steaphan asked as he stepped in and eyed us. "Looks it?"

Everyone nodded.

"Aye, great!" He beamed. "It's time to get started on our seven-day trip through the bonny Scottish Highlands. Today we're headin' to Oban, where we'll stay for a coupla days as we take side trips to Glencoe and Iona. As we drive, we'll stop for a wee break to stretch yer legs and take some photographs. Any questions?"

No one said anything. The two boys whispered furiously to each other, and both bounced in their seats. I chuckled.

"Excellent," Steaphan said. "And off we go!" He plunked himself down in the driver's seat, closed the doors, and rolled the bus away from the curb.

For the first half hour of our trip, I watched scenic Edinburgh fade away to the more rugged, rustic grounds of middle Scotland. I couldn't seem to get enough of the ancient beauty, the craggy green hills that seemed to pierce the low-lying clouds.

"Isn't it beautiful?" Mom said in a hushed tone as she leaned across the aisle toward me.

I nodded, unable to tear my gaze away. It almost looked unreal, it was so perfect. The sky was a rich, velvety blue, the grass brilliant green. Small clusters of sheep grazed and nibbled in far-off farmlands.

Mom and Dad talked in whispers to each other, and I found myself peering around the edge of the seat in front of me. I'd been trying to avoid looking at Graham, but I couldn't resist seeing what he was doing.

He was spun around in his seat, legs stretched in the aisle, talking with the lithe blond teen girl. His hands waved in front of him, and his face had that passionate look I'd come to recognize. Probably describing the wonders of Scotland to her. I couldn't help but smile at his enthusiasm.

I dug into my backpack and grabbed my sketchbook. The road we were traveling on was smooth, so I wanted to get a few rough sketches in during our downtime. I captured the lines of the jutting peaks of the distant mountains, a placid lake that reflected the blue sky, the tree-covered hills that rolled and danced along the way. More trees clustered along the bottoms of flattop crags.

Oh, a castle up ahead!

I fumbled and grabbed my phone to snap a couple of shots before it passed by. Then I kept the screen open as I started to sketch it. The stone bricks were moss-tinted and the top looked crumbled, with small, high windows. A stone wall ran along one side and wrapped around to the back. Thick clusters of trees spotted the grounds.

Beautiful. My brain went into the zone as my pencil swept across the paper. I wasn't even sure how much time had passed before the bus rolled to a stop. Oh, right—we were taking a rest break. I tucked my notebook and pencils into my bag.

"We'll stop here for the next half hour," Steaphan said as he stood and turned to our group. "Take yer time and walk around the grounds. Stretch yer legs. When ya return, we'll head right to Oban in time for a late lunch." He opened the doors, and the two families in front of us started to file off the bus.

I grabbed my backpack, looped it over my shoulder, and hopped off the bus. A stiff breeze whipped around the side of the bus, and I zipped my fleece up to my neck. Still, the sun was warm and shining, and the clouds were scattered and puffy. A fine day.

"Mom, I'm going over there to draw," I said as I pointed to a particularly lovely area where there was an abandoned castle in the near distance.

"Be careful," she said as she brushed a kiss across my brow.

I took a stiff step toward Graham, tempted to ask him to come along with me, but he was talking to the German family now, who peppered him with questions in stilted English. I didn't want to bother him when he was working, so I stepped into the grass and made my way over.

The air in this area was so fresh, unlike anything I'd ever smelled. It was pure, untainted, clean. I dragged several deep lungfuls in and smiled. Stretched my arms in glee.

Scotland was amazing.

I plopped down and grabbed my camera from my backpack. Corinne would die of jealousy when she saw my travel pictures. If these shots of the castle and hills didn't evoke the feel of Scotland and its rich history, nothing would. I focused in on the castle and snapped more shots. Vines and trees wove through holes and windows in the moss-covered stone.

How long had this place been abandoned? What was its history—who had lived here and then left? Maybe I should ask Graham later if he knew.

The sketch bug was itching at me again. I took out my notebook, flipped to a clean page, and began to draw. The only sounds were the light conversations of the fellow members of my group in the distance and the breezes floating by, rustling my hair and the leaves in the trees. Perfect serenity.

"That's a great rendering of the castle," a voice said from behind me.

My mouth curled into a smile before I even spun around and saw Graham standing there. "Thanks. I couldn't resist getting a few sketches of it while we took our break."

He sat down in the grass beside me and craned his neck to eye my sketches. Normally I wasn't that self-conscious about my art—I didn't need to be perfect, and I enjoyed the messiness of drafting—but I found myself eager for his approval and good opinion.

"Keep drawin'," he said. "Don't let me interrupt ya. We still have some time."

I kept my hand steady as I went back to roughing out the castle. "So do you know anything about its history?" I asked to help distract me from his magnetic presence. "Does it have a name? How old is it?"

"Not sure," he said, and the light burr of his voice, so close to my ear, sent little shivers down my spine. "Let's make it up."

I drew a thick black shadow within one of the windows. "Okay, I'll start. Um . . ." I dropped my pencil and studied the actual castle form, the age of the brick. "I think it's from the 1600s, so it's really old. The land all around here belonged to the owner of the castle, who was a great lord."

"Laird." He gave me a crooked grin. "That's what we'd call him."

"Laird, got it." I nodded and returned his smile. The sun glinted in his hair, and I had to fight the urge to touch it and see if it was as soft as it looked. "Um." I cleared my throat and felt my stupid cheeks start to burn. "The laird was a great warrior, and he built this castle for his bride."

His eyes flickered as he studied me. "Musta loved her a lot," he said quietly. "To give her such a place to live. She was probably a foreigner, from . . . France. He'd gone there on official clan business and came back with a bride."

"Love at first sight," I managed to say. My heart was thudding hard now. I could smell the warm, compelling scent of his soap, and it was super hard not to lean forward and breathe him in.

"Clacher Castle," he said. "That's its name. And he was Laird Clacher."

"So why did they leave?"

He paused and thought for a moment, and a brisk breeze whipped through and slipped under the neckline of my fleece. I shivered. "Are ya chilled?" he asked.

"No, no, I'm fine." I gave a reassuring smile.

"Time to go, son!" Steaphan hollered from the bus, his voice echoing across the hills.

Great timing. My mouth twisted in a wry grin as I packed up my pencils, notebook, and camera. Graham jumped up and offered me his hand, then pulled me to my feet. His fingers were warm, and he held my hand for a moment longer than was needed.

"Um." Now his cheeks tinted a slight pink, and my pulse stuttered. "We should get goin'. Don't want my da to leave us behind."

"Yeah, that castle probably doesn't have electricity or running water," I teased.

We walked toward the bus, and in a tone so quiet I almost didn't hear, Graham said, "She left."

"Sorry?" I turned to him and saw that his eyes reflected a bit of sadness.

"The castle. After a few years, his homesick bride left him to return to France, and he got tired of living there alone. That's why it was abandoned." With a polite nod, Graham waved me onto the bus, and I took reluctant steps toward my seat and sat back down.

My stomach was a tight knot as I chewed over what he'd said. Those words had sounded far too personal to be just made up. Was he trying to tell me something? Could this be about me . . . or had there been a personal wound in his life that he'd allowed me to glimpse?

I couldn't help myself. I wanted to know more about him. Everything about him. I couldn't stop thinking about him, and I knew it was a dumb idea to let myself start falling for him ... but the heart wanted what the heart wanted.

Mine wanted to be around him.

The bus pulled back onto the street toward Oban, and I lifted my chin and squared my shoulders. I still had another week here, and I was determined to enjoy it to its very end. Yes, I was going to be leaving, but I'd deal with that when the time came. In the meantime, I was going to just let this be what it was and see where it led. Have fun hanging out with Graham and relishing this chemistry between us instead of being afraid of it.

And hope against hope I could leave Scotland with my heart intact.

Chapter ● Nine

W e're here!" Steaphan declared as he rolled the bus to the front of a huge, gorgeous bed-and-breakfast right on the waterfront. The walls were thick gray stones that gave the building an old, solid feel. The windows were long and numerous and found on every floor. The brilliant sun sparkled along everything in sight, making the waterfront bright and glittery. The sidewalk to the B and B's front door was sprinkled on both sides with rich-toned flowers in every color and a closely trimmed lawn.

I bounced in my seat and laughed at myself when I saw the two kids doing the same. This place was to be our home for the next couple of nights—and it was stunning. I could hardly wait to go inside.

"This is MacKensie House," Dad explained as he leaned over

toward me. He took out a folded piece of paper. "It got great reviews online as one of the best bed-and-breakfasts in Oban."

Mom gathered her bag, and she and Dad stood to stretch their backs. We all filed off the bus.

"Tonight is a free night, so feel free to explore Oban on your own," Steaphan told our group. "Let's check in first and get settled. Remember, our expedition's leavin' tomorrow at nine, so be ready."

After the parents checked us in at the front desk, manned by a slender old man wearing a wool cap, we took our suitcases to our rooms. When Dad opened the door and I peeked inside, I paused.

"Where's the other bed?" There was only one in the room.

Dad turned to me with a grin. "The adjoining room has a sleeper sofa. You'll have your own space for the next couple of nights. But don't get used to it, princess. You just lucked out this time."

I fought the urge to roll my eyes and stepped in. The room had yellow wallpaper with tiny rows of flowers, and there was a private bathroom, which made me happy—I'd heard some of these places had group facilities. My room had a large purple sofa, which Dad helped me pull out, and we put the nearby folded pile of sheets and blankets on it to make my bed.

I grabbed a couple of days' worth of clothes and placed them into the bedside table. "Okay, I'm done," I declared as I headed back to their room. "Can we go walking around?" I was eager to explore this cute little harbor town.

Mom glanced at her watch. "Sure, we have time before dinner.

We're eating with Steaphan and Graham in this wonderful sea-food place that came highly recommended."

Well, that was a pleasant surprise. I had already planned to ask them if I could hang out with Graham tonight, so this made it easier.

She raised her eyebrow. "I assume you're okay with this arrangement."

I managed an even nod. "Sounds like a plan."

Dad checked the time on his cell phone. "Okay, I'll meet you guys at six in front of the restaurant."

"Where are you going?"

"There's a tour in an hour I signed up for to explore a scotch distillery. I figured you two wouldn't be that interested in it."

I laughed. "No, I'm perfectly happy to stroll and shop instead."

Mom and I walked through the narrow blue-wallpapered hallway down the steep stairs and stopped to look at the lobby once more. There was a golden floral print on the walls, and the arches above the halls and doorways were ornately carved and painted white. The whole place was quaint and cute.

"Okay, missy," she said when we stepped outside. The strong scent of seawater hit us, and the air was slightly cooler. "Where to?"

I shrugged and looked both ways down the street. We were smack-dab on the harbor front, and our street was lined with other bed-and-breakfasts, businesses, and stately homes. A stunning view. "Maybe toward the center of town, that way?" I pointed to the right.

We walked along the coastline, and I saw boats lazily drift on the water.

"So did you have fun hanging out with Mollie?" I asked Mom.

She beamed. "I can't remember the last time I've had this good of a time. It was like we'd only been apart a few days, not years and years."

"With a friendship like yours, I'm not surprised." I'd heard Mom talk about Mollie on and off since I was a little kid. They exchanged holiday cards, talked on the phone a few times a year, and stayed in regular contact. "I think Corinne and I will be like that too. Even when we graduate and go to college, we'll still be best friends."

She ruffled my hair. "I'm sure you will. You two have a real connection. How's she doing, by the way?"

I filled her in on what the art program had involved so far and how Corinne had been chosen to enter the prestigious contest. "So needless to say, you can imagine Corinne is a bit stressed about it."

"Yeah, she does have some . . . control issues," Mom teased with a wink. "Well, I'm sure it'll go fine. And that boy she's working with might help her loosen up a bit. Sounds like he's her total opposite. Could be good for her."

More than one night, Mom had seen Corinne at our house, curled up on the couch, her face lined with stress over all the stuff she had to get done.

"I think she likes this guy," I told her. "And she doesn't know how to handle it. Corinne's never really had time for guys before, and it's freaking her out a bit."

"I'm sure she'll find her way," Mom said sagely. "We all take different paths to get to the place that makes us happiest. She's a smart girl. She'll figure out how to deal with her emotions."

She turned to me, and the sunshine beamed down on her skin and hair. Huh, I couldn't remember the last time I'd seen Mom so relaxed and simply . . . happy. Guess we all needed this vacation more than we'd realized.

"Are you enjoying Scotland so far, honey?"

I reached an arm around her and squeezed her side. "It's amazing. I'm loving it."

We strolled in silence for a few minutes and eyed the quaint rows of houses and businesses tucked among the clusters of vibrant green trees. When we turned a corner and I looked up the hillside where Oban was nestled into, I gasped.

"Wow, what is that?" I nodded my head at the massive coliseum built into the top of the hill, overlooking all of Oban.

"Isn't that amazing?" She dug into her pocket and produced a piece of paper with tourist highlights—I'd bet a dollar Dad had printed that out for her. The thought made me grin. "According to this, that's McCaig's Tower. It was built in the 1800s. Let's walk up there and see it." The paper rippled and whipped in the breeze as she folded it back up and put it away.

We wove through the bustling streets, the smell of salt water and fish and food and greenery thick and heavy in the cooler harbor air. By the time we reached the top, I was a bit winded. The sight itself took the rest of my breath away.

It was a large circle of stone arches, and inside was a well-maintained garden. We stepped in and paused to gather our breaths and take in the view. There were a few people milling around inside, but it was quiet and peaceful up here.

I spun around in a circle to take it all in, then peered toward the harbor, and the panoramic view from up here was riveting. I could see for miles and miles, the countryside, the waterfront, the town below. "I should have brought my camera," I groaned. Still, I dug out my phone and took a few pictures with it.

Mom leaned in toward me, and I took some shots of us in there. When she pulled back, she smiled and tucked a strand of hair behind my ear. "You like him a lot, don't you?" she said quietly. "I've watched you guys together, and I don't remember the last time I've seen you like this."

I nodded and gave a heavy sigh. We wandered the circumference of the tower. "Yeah, but he's kind of driving me crazy. One minute it seems like he likes me a lot. The next, he's keeping me at arm's length."

"Maybe because you two live so far apart," she mused. "Though I have to say, that's normal for guys." Her eyes danced. "Your father did the same to me when we first started talking. I actually thought he liked one of my friends for the longest time, so it shocked me when he asked me out."

"I'm glad it worked out between you two," I said drolly, "or else I wouldn't be here right now, enjoying the scenery."

She chuckled and bumped my shoulder. "Very funny. But seriously, I want you to be careful. I'm not sure how smart it is to fall in love with a guy who lives so far away. It's one thing if it's just a fun crush, but another when your heart gets involved."

"You and Mollie stayed in touch," I pointed out. "And like you said, it was like you guys hadn't been apart that long."

"Friendship is different. Relationships come with their own pressure. I just . . . don't want to see you get hurt." She pressed a kiss to my forehead and moved off toward the center of the gardens.

I stuck around the edges and absorbed her words. I knew what her concern was—after David had dumped me, I'd holed up in my room crying for days. It had hurt so badly, because I'd seen it coming and could do nothing to stop it.

David was charming, handsome. Around school he'd started paying me more and more attention, and I hadn't been able to believe it at first. But then when I'd accepted it was real, or so I'd thought, I let all my walls down and opened up to him.

Which was fine at first, until out of nowhere he started pulling away. Not returning all of my calls, then not returning any of them. Not seeking me out between classes in school, then avoiding me altogether. Only wanting to hang out when it was convenient for him, then not seeing me at all.

When he'd finally broken up with me, the truth had been clear—I'd liked him far more than he'd liked me.

I sighed and turned to face the water again, giving myself time to tuck that flash of pain back into the recesses of my chest. It didn't hurt because I still liked him. No, I'd gotten over that and moved on. The pain was because I'd fooled myself into thinking we'd felt the same way. I'd vowed not to do that. I wouldn't put everything on the line unless someone was willing to do the same. The guy I dated next would have to put in as much effort as I did.

I'd been too embarrassed to tell anyone why we'd broken up, my pride singed, my heart too raw. But Graham was starting to crack my heart open with his humor and intelligence and smiles, and I couldn't help but like him. Despite my hesitations.

All I could do was hope that when this week was over, I could walk away happy we'd had this time together. Not crying because I wanted more.

"Dinner was perfect," I said as I pushed my plate away. I rubbed my full belly. "That fish was unbelievable." I'd devoured the halibut, flaky and seasoned with a tangy rub, not realizing how hungry I'd been until I'd started eating it. The potatoes and fresh vegetables had been the perfect complements.

Graham smiled. "Mine was too." He'd gotten scallops drizzled in a cream sauce and had eaten almost as fast as I had.

Our parents were talking, and had been since we'd arrived for dinner. The whole time, Graham and I had exchanged shy glances across the long table. There was definitely something between us; several times I could feel his gaze on me and would look up to meet his eyes.

I peered out the large windows to the harbor front; the sun washed over the sky in dark pinks, purples, and blues. As I dropped my fidgeting fingers into my lap, I was filled with a sudden urge to breathe in the early evening air.

I cleared my throat and faced Graham again. His blue eyes were locked on me, his mouth curved in a slight smile. "Wanna go walk a bit?" I asked him.

His shrug was casual. "Sure, sounds fine." Despite the easygoing nature of his words and gesture, I could see a spark of interest in his gaze.

"Dad," I whispered once there was a small lull in their conversation. "Can Graham and I walk around on the waterfront? We'll stay on this street."

He narrowed his eyes a fraction, and I knew exactly what he was thinking.

"Come on, don't make them listen to our boring adult conversation," Mom teased him.

He sniffled, then nodded. "Fine, but be back here in a half hour, on the dot."

I jumped up before he could change his mind and kissed his cheek. "Thanks. We will!"

We headed outside, and the air was brisk and tinged with salt. Stars peppered the eastern side of the sky. I couldn't help but smile at the view. It was a lovely town.

"So, do you like being a tour guide?" I asked Graham. "That must keep you busy when you're not in school."

His arm brushed mine, and I tried to ignore the nervous flutter in my belly. "Aye, I do. I know a lot about my country. I'm proud of that. And my da works hard to provide a good experience to our guests."

"What's your favorite place to visit on this tour?"

He turned to face me, and his eyes twinkled in the dim light. "It's a surprise. You'll see. Can't wait to show ya."

Well, that sounded promising. I crooked a smile. "I can't wait, then."

The silence stretched comfortably for a minute or two as we both listened to birds cawing and the light conversation of couples and families around us. Shop fronts glowed with a warm yellow light, casting bright splashes of color in the dimming skies.

"I bet you meet people from all over the world," I finally said. "That has to be neat. How many languages do you know?"

"English, some Gaelic, a wee bit of French. Though my French isn't that great," he admitted. "You?"

"I'm taking Spanish in school. I'd love to go to Mexico someday, but I imagine my school Spanish is quite different from living Spanish." A group of birds bounced along the sidewalk in front of us. "Do you meet a lot of Americans?"

"Some."

"A lot of American girls?" I teased.

A pause. Then, "Aye, some."

"I hope they're at least nice and not giving my country a bad name."

He stiffened, and my chest tightened a fraction. "For the most part, Americans are excited about touring our countryside. We get people like your family who are seeking information about their heritage. . . ." His voice trailed off. "Met a girl last summer who took our tour."

There was a thread of emotion in his voice, almost wistfulness or sadness. I couldn't quite tell. "Sounds like it didn't end well."

"No, it didn't."

I started to ask what happened, but before I could, he turned to me with a broad smile and said, "Wanna look in this gift shop? Might find something to finish off yer shopping."

Okay, message received loud and clear. I pasted on a big grin of my own and nodded. "Yeah, we have a few minutes before we have to go back. And I still have to find a gift for my friend back home." I followed him inside, trying not to focus on all the questions roaring in my head.

It was obvious what had happened. An American girl had broken his heart. But who was she, and what had she done? Was that why he was so hot and cold around me—because of her? My mind flashed back to our earlier conversation, our story about the castle. As I stared at the case of necklaces, my heart sank.

The French bride in the castle—she must have been this other American girl. And given the way he'd changed the subject, it was all too possible that she still had some part of his heart.

Chapter ● Ten

The strong morning breezes whipped and tore through my hair, and I clutched the side of the ferry with a tighter grip. A cluster of clouds gathered in the distance and seemed to be moving west at a steady clip—right toward us. Well, we'd had several days of glorious sunshine. Couldn't last forever.

"This crazy wind is going to blow me right off the ferry!" I called out to my mom with a laugh.

She grinned, and her hair danced in the air too. "At least we're here and you can walk to the shore if you fall off the boat."

Our ferry docked, and our tour group exited. I eyed the small island for a moment, the homes and ancient buildings that speckled the green landscape.

Steaphan waved us to the side. His turtleneck was a rich

purple that made his dark hair shine and his light skin glow. We all had on rain jackets, as we'd been warned about the possibility of drizzling weather today. "We have a coupla hours to explore the island. It's a wee size, so don't worry about getting lost. Only two kilometers by six kilometers or so." He winked at me with a cheeky grin. "That's a mile wide by around four miles long for you Americans."

I chuckled and nodded my thanks. Yeah, my metric conversions were a bit on the slow side.

"Population of Iona is small, under a hundred and fifty or so. But it's a bonny isle. Make sure ya check out the abbey while you're here. It's well worth the visit to see the architectural details, and the main building itself has great historical importance as one of the best-preserved abbeys to survive the Middle Ages." He glanced at his watch. "Okay, meet back here at eleven thirty. We'll ferry back to Oban for lunch, then head to Glencoe for the afternoon. All right?"

Our families all nodded, and the Swedish family came up and started talking to him.

The two little German kids tugged at their mom's hands and pulled her toward the shore, where they grabbed sticks and started carving into the rocky sand. She stood back and watched them with a bemused smile. I laughed—I was so the same way when I was little, wanting to get dirty and make mud pies all the time.

"Sometimes I miss being that carefree," Graham said, popping up beside me, his eyes on the kids.

"Me too. Though I'd hate to come all the way to Iona just to play with dirt." I eyed the landscape, the rugged hills both on the tiny island and on the faraway mainland shore that had come to represent the heart and soul of Scotland to me. Hard to believe this was my seventh day in this country. In some ways, it felt like I'd been here for weeks. In others, the time had passed like a blink of an eye.

"Wanna hit the abbey with me?" he asked.

I nodded and couldn't fight the excitement building in my chest. He'd sought me out and wanted to walk with me. I darted over to my parents, who waved me off with a knowing shake of their heads. Apparently, they weren't worried about me getting lost, since the island was so small. They threaded their fingers together and walked off.

Graham and I strolled across a flower-dotted stretch of grass toward a series of stone buildings in the near distance. The clouds had begun to thicken and stretch out over us, so the sunlight dappled in small bursts across the grass.

He cleared his throat. "Look, I want to apologize for last night. I was . . . a wee abrupt, and I'm sorry."

Our evening had ended in a stilted manner, with neither of us really looking at each other and both wearing these big, fake smiles. I'd felt too embarrassed to press him for more information, especially since it was clear he didn't want to talk about it. And he'd gotten quiet and pulled away. Last night it had taken me a while to fall asleep, my stomach was so nervous about what would happen today.

I gave him a nod. "Thanks," I replied sincerely. Though a hint of that awkwardness was still lingering, I was glad he'd come to me to talk about it. "I didn't mean to be nosy, Graham—"

"No, it's not you," he said, shaking his head. "It's . . . well, if ya don't mind, I'd rather not talk about it today." He bent down and plucked a small yellow flower out of the ground. "Is that all right?" With a small smile of apology, he handed me the flower.

"Oh, sure." I couldn't quite blame him. Sometimes talking about the past soured the mood of the present. And today, on this tiny island, I wanted to enjoy my time, not pollute it with bad memories. "I get it, trust me. It's totally fine." I tucked a lock of my hair behind my ear, then added the flower.

"Bonny," he said as he eyed me. There was a hint of a smile on his face.

My cheeks burned. There was no doubt he wasn't just talking about the flower. He meant me. I swallowed and gave him a nervous grin.

We headed toward the abbey, our steps slow and purposeful. No rushed movements, just a leisurely walk. The tension in my chest from earlier lightened with each step. Yes, Graham might have liked a girl in his past, and I couldn't control or impact that. But he wasn't with her now, that much was obvious. He'd even told me before that he was single.

Instead of being worried about his past and how it impacted me, I should focus on the here and now. Enjoy these moments we had together.

We neared the group of buildings, which had a small graveyard on the side. There were people already wandering around, eyeing the headstones, entering and exiting buildings.

Graham pressed a hand to my lower back, which sent a surge of warmth into my torso. He guided me to the edge of the graveyard. "All right, lemme see if I recall my da's speech."

I chuckled. "I'm sure you'll do a fine job."

He cleared his throat and began in an overly formal manner, mimicking his father's deep voice, "In case you weren't aware, a number of Scottish kings were buried in the abbey grounds in the past."

I bit back a giggle.

"In fact," he said, waving his hand with a finger pointed in the air as I'd seen his dad do, "a few kings of other countries like Norway and Ireland are buried here as well. Wouldn't have expected that, would ya?"

"That's super interesting," I said as seriously as I could manage.

His eyes twinkled as he looked at me. "Did I do a fair enough job?"

"More than."

"Then let's move on, because that's all I can remember," he said as he waved his hand toward the cluster of buildings. "Follow me, please."

More clouds moved in, and the sun was blotted out completely as we headed into the actual chapel. While we walked around, admiring the columns, the ancient stone, and the religious solemnity of the area, Graham told me about the history of the chapel, dating back to the twelfth century. Whereas he'd been a little silly outside, in here his hushed tones showed his true feelings—filled with respect and honor for this island's importance.

I couldn't help but watch, transfixed, while he moved around, showed me the interior of the chapel. His words spilled in excitement as he relayed information his dad had told him, memories he had of visiting here as a kid.

We left the abbey, quieter than we'd been before, and walked in a gentle silence as the air misted and drizzled around us. I pulled my hood over my hair so it wouldn't be a frizzy mess. By unspoken agreement, we drifted toward the rocky waterfront, listening as birds cawed and the water lapped the shores. Despite the weather, there was a serenity on this small island I hadn't expected.

"Do you come here often?" I asked him, then flushed when I realized how cheesy and clichéd that sounded.

Luckily, he didn't seem to pick up on the double entendre. "I pretty much only come during tours. And I'm usually too busy helping my da to enjoy it. Since our group is small this time, the experience is different."

We stared out at the water, and I took mental pictures of the panoramic skyline. The water had grown darker and choppier as the wind picked up; I shivered as a brisk breeze whipped a spray of water along my neck.

Graham stepped in front of me to block me from the rain, which started to pound harder and slant at an angle. "We should find somewhere to go and dry off," he said in a husky tone as he looked down at me. His eyes seemed to have changed with the weather, slightly hooded and darker than I'd seen them. He pulled my hood over my head a little tighter.

I sucked in a shaky breath as I inched closer to him. There were scant inches separating us now, and my blood hummed in my veins. I wanted this guy to kiss me so badly I could almost taste it. Water beaded on his eyelashes, dribbled down his face and hair. "You're getting soaked." My voice sounded throaty.

Long moments passed, and he glanced at my mouth. Inched a fraction closer. Then blinked and moved back, giving a shaky smile. The hesitation was clear in his eyes, his stiff body language. "Let's get back inside the chapel till this passes over."

I scraped together my pride and nodded like I was a bobble-head doll. "Yeah, sure. Totally."

We ran all the way back to the chapel, rain drumming on our heads, our backs. My feet slipped in a few muddy spots, and Graham grabbed my hand to steady me before I fell. When we got inside, we saw clusters of others doing the same thing, peering out the small windows and waiting the weather out. The German dad waved at Graham to come over to them.

"I'll be back in a moment," he told me with an apologetic smile.

"Yeah, that's totally fine. Go ahead." I urged him away. That was good anyway, because I kind of needed to pull emotionally back into myself. I'd been about three seconds from leaning toward him and planting a kiss right on his mouth.

Which would have been a total disaster, given the way he'd moved back. I'd either really misread his face or he'd changed his mind and decided he didn't want to kiss me after all.

Pride burned low in my gut. It would have crushed me to see him regretful about it. Not to mention make the rest of the trip awkward.

I kept my gaze firmly focused outside and waited for the rain to lighten. After about ten minutes, Graham came back to my side, and in another few minutes, the rain became a light drizzle again. Good enough for Scottish standards—we could continue walking around.

I kept my hands tucked in my jacket pocket and my distance far enough away to keep me from looking clingy. I smiled and laughed at his jokes, kept the game face on to not give away my embarrassment about our non-kiss. We boarded the ferry, and I rejoined my parents and summed up what I'd learned about Iona.

I was proud of myself for not looking back at Graham once.

Glencoe was unreal.

Our group was in the actual glens of Glencoe, having spent a little time first exploring the nearby quaint village. Steaphan had informed us the population there was just over three hundred, and the homes were tucked neatly into the hillside, with a clean stretch of road down the middle. Given that I lived in a popular suburb of Cleveland with over fifty thousand people in just under seven square miles, I found it amazing that people lived in such small towns.

Steaphan gathered us around and told us the story of what had happened here in 1692, the massacre of innocent people that haunted Glencoe's residents even today. I pressed a hand to my chest, moved by the passion and sorrow etched on Steaphan's face as he talked.

"This is sad, yah?" the Swedish girl said in a hushed whisper to me.

I blinked in surprise. "Um, yes, it really is." She'd hardly looked at me since we'd started our trip yesterday morning, though I'd tried to tell her hello before. Given that we were the only two teenage girls on the trip, I was glad she was making the effort now. Maybe she was just shy.

As Steaphan talked on, she told me, "I am Tilda." She thrust her hand out to me, and her cheeks flushed with a light-pink color. "My English is no good sometimes. But I still try. So I wanted to be saying hello."

Ah, so self-consciousness about her language skills was why she hadn't been much of a talker. My heart welled with sympathy for her. It was hard, risking being laughed at. I took her hand and shook it. "You speak better English than I speak any other language," I assured her with a smile. "I'm Ava."

"You like Scotland, yah?" she spoke slowly, as if thinking on each word before saying it. "And the island this morning, it was . . . pretty."

I nodded and slowed my speech a bit to make it easier for her to translate. "Yes, it's beautiful. I keep thinking I can't be surprised anymore, but with every new site we visit, I'm shocked by its beauty. I've probably taken a hundred pictures so far, and we still have several days left in our tour."

"Yah, me too." She gave a light chuckle and tucked her dark-blond hair behind her ear. Her eyes danced with unreserved warmth. "I am glad we are talking, Ava. Maybe we can talk later too?"

"That would be great." My smile matched hers.

"Okay, I am joining my family now. I will see you!" She bounced off to her mom and dad's sides, and I heard the soft tones of their Swedish tongue.

After Steaphan finished his lecture on the history of Glencoe, we milled around the area on our own, and I grabbed my camera. The drizzle had finally let up, though the clouds still threatened overhead to burst any time. There was no way I wasn't going to capture the majestic mountain ranges around us, though. I snapped off several shots of the ragged mountains, some in the distance even crested with ice and snow at their very tips. The clouds didn't detract from their beauty. Nature rustled around me, the wind dancing across the greens.

When I tucked my camera away, I heard Graham talking to the German family about how many movies had scenes shot here in Glencoe. The lilt of his native Scottish tongue rolled and danced, and the kids gasped when they realized that parts of a wildly popular children's movie had been filmed here. As Graham beamed down at them, my heart clutched tight.

I'd kept away from him at lunch—subtly, of course. I didn't want him to think I was avoiding him. I just . . . needed time to not feel so much around him. To not want him as badly as I did.

Because that near kiss had opened my eyes to the truth. As crazy as it was, I was falling in love with Scotland. And with Graham. I could tell myself it was a simple vacation crush, and I could pretend to my family like it didn't matter.

But it did. He mattered to me. When our week ended and my trip was over, I didn't want to tell him good-bye.

And I had no idea what to do with that realization . . . or how to go about convincing Graham to give me a chance.

Chapter • Eleven

Rise and shine, princess!" Dad said as he shook my shoulder.

I yawned and eyed him with a sleepy glare as I shoved my messy hair out of my face. "It's not time to get up yet, is it?" The pale gray light slanting through the window told me was early morning. Really early.

"Unfortunately, it is. We're driving to Loch Ness this morning, and this afternoon will be a visit to the Highland Games! Isn't that great?" he declared as he tugged the blanket off my curled-up figure. "It's going to be a busy day for our group. Breakfast first, though. It should be excellent today."

I had to admit, our B and B owner could cook a mean breakfast. Her eggs were the fluffiest I'd ever had in my life. My stomach gave an involuntary growl, and Dad shot me a knowing look.

"Gimme a half hour to get ready," I told him with a laugh. Now that I was starting to wake up, the excitement about our day's trip hit me fully. I jumped out of bed and showered as fast as possible. A peek outside confirmed it was overcast still but not rainy, so I wore jeans, boots, and a long-sleeved shirt with my rain jacket. Since my hair was likely going to be a frizz fest if I didn't wrestle it under control, I used bobby pins to secure the sides and minimize damage.

I'd packed my bags last night, so I tucked my toiletries in and readied myself for leaving this B and B. When we got to Inverness, we were checking into another inn, where we'd stay for a couple of days.

Mom was sitting on the edge of her bed, flipping through a Scotland tourism magazine. She stood. "Ready to go?"

"Where's Dad?"

She snorted. "Take a guess."

I shook my head with a wry smile. "Never mind. Let's go meet him—he probably has a table already for us . . . and might have finished his food at this point." Dad was pretty infamous for being unable to patiently wait. If we were shopping, he was three stores ahead. When Mom was getting dressed, he almost always already had her coffee poured and was working on his second cup.

My stomach gave a nervous pitch as we entered the dining room, a cozy blue-walled place with several small tables scattered around. Graham was up and working on his eggs at a table with his dad on the other side of the room. Our eyes connected, and my heart stuttered.

It should be illegal for him to be this handsome. His shirt was a dark-red slim-fit that accented his muscled upper arms and chest.

He gave me a friendly nod, and I returned it. I could totally do this—get through the day without blurting out my growing romantic feelings for him. No problem. Mom and I sat at our table, and the B and B owner, a kindly older woman with a tight gray perm, brought us today's menu with our choices.

My toast, eggs, and salmon came quickly, and I almost inhaled them. Man, that woman could cook. I spent the meal talking with my parents about today's morning trip to Loch Ness, whether we'd actually see the monster . . . if it was even possible for the monster to exist. When Tilda came into the dining room with her family, I made sure to give her a big wave, which she returned with a broad smile.

Finally we loaded our luggage, boarded the bus, and pulled away to head to the road leading to Loch Ness. I popped a piece of gum in my mouth and chewed as I stared out at the passing scenery. Everything around here was coated in a rich, lush green, despite all the jutting rocks.

I pressed my forehead to the glass and let the scene fly by my unfocused eyes. Just relaxed into the moment and enjoyed the ambient noise around me: my parents talking in low whispers, the German kids—who I learned yesterday were named Karl and

Lucas—giggling with their parents, Tilda and Graham discussing yesterday's trip to Glencoe.

Before I knew it, a hand was shaking my shoulder. "Ava, we're here," Graham's voice rumbled close to my ear.

I blinked and looked at him through sleep-foggy eyes. "Oh my God, did I fall asleep?" I gave an embarrassed laugh, trying not to focus on the sensation of that firm hand warming my skin through my thin shirt.

"Aye, but I've fallen asleep on long rides too," he said with a smile. "Don't feel bad." He held his hand out to me, and I took it as he tugged me out of my seat. The rest of the bus had already emptied out. Whoops. I must have been more tired this morning than I'd realized.

I grabbed my backpack and followed him off the bus. My mom had a light smile on her face as she shook her head at me. Dad glanced at his watch, most likely because he was ready to get this tour started.

"Gather round," Steaphan said as he waved at all our families; we stood near the bus, which blocked my view of the lake. "I chose this spot for us to explore Loch Ness this morn because it's the best place to see it in its full beauty. We have a coupla hours here before moving on to Inverness. So take some time to soak it in."

Steaphan took a moment to explain that Loch meant "lake" in Scottish, so Loch Ness was just one of many lakes Scotland boasted. It stretched over twenty miles, and our current location was just north of the middle. He told us a little more about its history and importance.

"And if yer lucky, ya just might see"—Steaphan paused and eyed Karl and Lucas—"the Loch Ness monster!"

Their dad tickled the boys' sides as he quickly translated Steaphan's words, and they squealed and jumped.

My parents stood near each other, and my dad wrapped his arm around my mom's waist. She melted into his side, sighed, and pressed a kiss to his cheek. I glanced away—not because they were my parents, but because the sight of such open affection made me a little jealous. I wanted that too.

I shook off that momentary melancholy and walked over to them. We stepped away from the bus, and I got my first impressive view of the lake. It was massive, surrounded by lush mountains. The sky stretched on forever. I was happy to see the clouds beginning to move away from us, so sunlight sparkled and danced on the water.

A perfect image. My brain was itching to get creative.

"I'm going to take some pictures and draw, if you guys want to walk around a bit," I told them as I pointed to a nearby knoll. It would give me an ideal spot to capture the water's beauty.

Mom frowned. "Are you sure?"

I waved them off with a heavy fake sigh. "Seriously, go. Spend some private time together. I'll be fine, promise. I'll stay within eyesight of the van. And I have my phone," I said as I tapped my front left pocket.

Dad pressed a kiss to my brow. "If you change your mind, we'll be wandering this way." He indicated the shoreline heading north toward a nearby castle.

"Thanks. Have fun, you two."

Dad cupped Mom's elbow and led her away, and I chuckled as they strolled. Those two were so different, but they were still madly in love. It gave me hope that someday I might have that too.

I scanned the grounds and saw Graham talking to Tilda and her family off in the distance. He was pointing at the castle, probably doing work stuff, so I didn't want to bother him. I made my way to the grassy patch, stretched my jacket out on the ground, and sat down.

For the first couple of minutes I just . . . absorbed. Opened all my senses to take the scene fully in. Birds chirped in nearby clusters of trees. The wind sighed as it swept across the water. The air was clean, fresh, pure—no salty tinge, since Loch Ness was a freshwater lake.

The lake itself looked like a deep, straight cleft in the mountain range. How had it been made? If I saw Steaphan, I'd make sure to ask him.

I grabbed my notebook and began to draw, letting my pencil fly across the paper. Big, rough lines to capture the hills, the smooth water's surface, the castle thrusting off the side of the cliff in a crumbling beauty.

After doing a few sketches, I grabbed my camera and began snapping shots of the view. In my head I was already envisioning a sort of panoramic image, comprised of overlapping pictures, that could stretch along one wall of my bedroom. So I made sure each shot was careful and even.

When I reached the north side with my photos, I saw Graham still talking with Tilda. I zoomed in and snapped a picture of his face, the sunlight peeking through clouds and illuminating his skin. His eyes glowed bright blue, the same shade as the water behind him.

I took another picture, tilted my camera on end, and got a long shot.

At that moment, Graham turned from Tilda, and his gaze locked on me. I swallowed and dropped my camera. Crud! Totally busted. Despite the roar in my ears from my flaring pulse, I gave him a jaunty wave and pretended like I wasn't mortified.

He stepped away from Tilda and strolled toward me. When he was a few feet away, he glanced down at the open sketchbook resting on my jacket. "Lovely," he said. "Ya captured the spirit of Loch Ness."

"Thanks." I flushed with pleasure. "Um. So . . . dumb question, but . . . is it possible that the Loch Ness monster could be real?"

His mouth crooked in a grin. "Anything's possible, I suppose. But science doesn't seem to support it. My da says the lake was formed ten thousand years ago because of glaciers melting. Not old enough for Nessie, an ancient sea creature, to be trapped in her waters." He shrugged. "Still, it's a harmless bit o' fun."

"You know everything," I said as I shook my head in admiration.

"I also know the best view of Loch Ness. Come with me."

My heart fluttered at those words, the simple invitation. I scrambled to cram my belongings back in my bag and slipped beside Graham as we headed north.

When we approached the castle, he presented the tickets.

"I figured ya might want to see it," he said with a casual shrug. "It's an important castle because it's so old, and I know ya like the old sites."

The air froze in my lungs, and it took me a moment to say, "Thank you. That's really nice of you."

He'd planned this ahead of time to surprise me? Just me—not anyone else on the tour. My hands trembled, and I stuffed them into my jacket pockets.

We explored the tower house first, weaving through small groups of tourists who snapped pictures and pointed at various spots of ruins. Graham explained that the castle originated in the late 500s. Hard to believe I was standing in a spot nearing fifteen hundred years old.

"Back then, this was a five-story building. There was a great storm in the 1700s that collapsed that south wall," he said as he indicated the ruins. "But ya can still see what it might have been like back then."

After a few minutes, we left the tower and explored the grounds. I brushed my fingers along the stone rubble walls. This place had to be something when it had been in its prime. There was one higher hill with a flag, which we climbed to. Once we reached it, we spun around, and I was able to take in a glorious view of the lake.

"Wow," I breathed. "This is unreal." He was right about it being the ultimate view. I took some photographs and then impulsively said, "Would you take a picture with me?"

After blinking, he said, "Oh. Aye, sure."

We turned around so the lake was behind us, and I angled my camera to get us in the frame. I snapped the shot, then used the viewfinder to preview the image.

"Wow, that went badly," I said with a giggle as I showed it to him. The picture was just the crowns of our heads, the lake tilted at an odd angle in the background.

He huffed a laugh. "Aye, a bit of a disaster, that was. Maybe we should take another. Try tilting the camera down until ya can see yer face in the lens. And make sure to keep it level."

We tried again, me angling it based on his suggestion, and this time the picture was exactly right. My heart thudded almost painfully at the sight of our two heads tucked closely together, the lake sprawled out in a glorious blue behind us, reflecting the sky and mountains. The smile stretching his face reflected his relaxation, and his eyes glinted with pure happiness.

Wow. Being with me made him look that way.

I checked out my face in the picture and realized I bore the exact same grin as him, the same evident happiness. No big surprise there.

I didn't want to look weird staring at our photo, so I put the camera away after thanking him for taking the picture with me. I knew I'd most likely be checking it out again in the near future, when I could allow myself the luxury of studying his face.

"So did you ever believe in Nessie?" I asked him as we peered out toward the water.

He chuckled and pushed his sleeves up his forearms. "Aye, as a young lad I did, until I was around seven or eight. For a while, I was even determined to prove she was real. I made my da bring me to the loch during the summer, and I'd sit on the shore for hours, binoculars in hand. Just waiting for her to pop up. Though honestly, I don't know what I'da done if she had. Probably screamed or cried."

I snorted. "I would have too. So what made you decide she wasn't real? Was it because you never saw her?"

"As I got older, I watched a few documentaries with irrefutable evidence against her existence." He leaned in close, and the light caught the blue of his eyes. "Still, nothing wrong with a little hope, right?"

I nodded, swallowed. Hope was a living thing in my heart—hope that Graham was feeling this connection as strongly as I was. I'd told myself I wasn't going to plunge headfirst into this . . . thing with him. Yet here I was, finding myself unable to stop staring into his eyes.

So much for my self-proclaimed ability to maintain my distance. I gave a mental head shake. Still, it was hard to do so when Graham was opening up to me, letting me into his world. And that picture was pretty good evidence I wasn't alone in this feeling. That kind of earnestness couldn't be faked.

"Did ya have beliefs as a kid?" he asked me.

I rubbed my fingers along the stone wall at my right side. "I believed in *everything* when I was little. I would stay up late, waiting for fairy lights in the big tree right outside my bedroom window. I even swore I saw unicorns in the woods." I bit my lip and huffed a breath of laughter. "To their credit, my parents didn't try to cram reality down my throat. They let me explore. They fostered my creativity."

He nodded. "I like yer parents, Ava. They're good people."

"They really are." I was so lucky. In this moment, I realized once again how fortunate I was. Happy home life, on a vacation of a lifetime, talking with a handsome boy.

Graham nodded toward the water. "Yanno, this place always felt magical to me, even if it was just a fairy tale." He glanced at me, his eyes open and honest. "That sounds silly, I'm sure. A guy talkin' 'bout fairies and such."

"No, it doesn't." I leaned toward him. "There's this park near our neighborhood where I like to walk sometimes. The path winds through the trees, and you just feel . . . connected to your surroundings. How is that not magical?"

"I believe it is." He reached over and brushed my forearm, and my throat tightened. "Can't wait to show ya my favorite spot tomorrow. If anyone will feel the magic there, it'll be you."

I couldn't wait either.

Chapter Twelve

The bus ride to Inverness didn't take long. It helped that the Highland views out my window were captivating. I wasn't sure I'd ever get tired of seeing those craggy hills, the moss-covered stones, the mountains that roared to the sky and punctured the clouds.

And the views inside the bus were pretty compelling too. My gaze was drawn back to Graham's profile again and again, and I drank it in. Imprinted it to memory—the high cheekbones, the straight line of his nose, the firm jaw. That small dimple that popped in his cheek when he grinned.

Every conversation I had with Graham made me connected to him even more. I couldn't stop thinking of him as a cute black-haired boy, running around Loch Ness hoping to find evidence of Nessie. It made my heart squeeze with delight. Not to mention how cool it was that he and I were so alike.

I'd never imagined there were guys like him in the world. Then again, I'd had to travel over three thousand miles to meet him.

"How did you like Loch Ness?" Mom asked me. "Can I see your sketches?"

I grabbed them from my bag and showed her. She oohed and aahed as she flipped from page to page. Dad peered over her shoulder and gave me a nod of approval.

"You did a great job," Mom gushed. "I like how you captured the movement in the trees across the water. I can tell your skill is improving."

"Thanks." I beamed from their praise. Summertime was great for giving me the extra time to work on my craft. During the school year, I didn't have much time to simply sit at my easel for hours.

Steaphan navigated the bus to a parking lot, then pulled to a stop and stood. "We're here! I think yer gonna enjoy today's festivities. The Highland Games are an important part of Scottish culture. Let's go watch some caber tossing and get fish-and-chips, aye? When that's done, we'll check into our inn. This evening is free time to explore Inverness on yer own."

One by one we got off the bus. Excitement rippled in the air as crowds made their way toward the park, and I heard music and cheers and talking pouring from all around. I saw tents set up along one side, and tourists laden with cameras who milled around the grounds. The sun was out in full force, with wispy clouds off in the distance. I tied my jacket around my waist and pushed up my sleeves. Beautiful afternoon weather.

"We're lucky to be around when Inverness is hosting their Highland Games," Mom explained. "They only do it one day a year. Should be a lot of fun!"

Our tour group filed toward the entrance with the rest of the crowd, and Steaphan paid our entry fee. By unspoken agreement, we all stuck together—funny how a couple of days made us feel connected. Graham was talking to my parents, and while I couldn't understand what he was saying over the crowd noise, I still watched him for a moment, drawn to the light in his eyes and dimple in his cheek. Then I turned my focus to the site before me.

Whoa.

The area was a large open field with portions bracketed off. A long row of young girls dressed in their finest dancing clothes were currently kicking and swinging their legs. Their arms were thrust in the air as they danced proudly. People in the crowd clapped and cheered, and the bagpipes roared and lilted.

Our group moved to an area that wasn't as crowded and observed the dance competition. The girls wore a look of concentration on their faces; their bright-colored kilts bounced with every kick of their legs.

I took out my camera and grabbed some action shots. With the sun pouring across the field, everything was illuminated perfectly.

"Your mom and I are going to grab food," my dad said. "Hungry?"

"I'm still full from breakfast," I told him, turning my camera on its side to take portrait-framed photos. "I'll stay right here, okay?" I knew with the crowds this large, my parents would want me to hang out with our group.

"Okay, we'll be back soon!" Mom and Dad waved and left toward the food tents.

I put my camera away and hung close behind Tilda and her folks, who were speaking rapidly and pointing at the dancers. When Tilda saw me, she beamed and moved back to my side.

"Hello, Ava! This is great, yah?"

I nodded. "I could never dance like this. I'm not nearly coordinated enough." At her frown, I rephrased, "I'm very clumsy. I trip a lot."

"Oh, I see." Her eyes twinkled with laughter. "Yah, I love to dance. But . . . I have never danced like that."

"What kind of dancing do you do?"

"I am . . . modern dancer, I think is how you say."

I blinked in surprise. "Really? How cool! I took dance lessons when I was a kid, but I was very, very bad. My mom finally stopped making me do it."

When I was five, I'd watched some old dance movies and decided I wanted to learn how to do that. Mom signed me up for six months of dance lessons . . . where I found out that (a) I was far too uncoordinated to ever look graceful at dancing, and (b) the practice was really, really boring and repetitive for me. No, dancing wasn't my thing, but I could appreciate the art and beauty for those who did it well.

Graham's laugh hit my ears, and I turned my head automatically toward it. His teeth flashed as he threw his head back and chortled at something his dad said.

"You . . . like him, right?" Tilda said in a low voice to me.

My first instinct was to downplay my crush. I gave a casual shrug. "Sure, he's a really nice guy."

Her lips quirked. "Yah, he is. And . . . very handsome too."

The music ended, and the crowd broke out in cheers and claps. I joined in, as did Tilda. The winning dancers were announced, and we applauded the girl who won first place, who had tears in her eyes and a broad smile on her sweaty face.

The dancers left, and I saw a row of guys in shorts and tank tops start stretching. Must be time for track events.

I kept my face neutral, aimed toward the field, and answered, "Yes, he is very handsome." Heart thudding, I continued, "I do have a little crush on him. Not that anything is going to happen with it, of course."

"Why not?" Tilda sounded genuinely confused.

I looked at her and saw that confusion in her eyes. "Because he lives here and I live in America."

"And you have no phone or computer in America?" There was a teasing lilt in her voice.

I chuckled. "Yes, I do, but . . ." Anxiety knotted my stomach, and I took a step toward her so I could speak in a lower voice. "I can't tell how he feels. I think he likes me too, but it might not be as much as I like him. And I don't want to get hurt again, caring about someone who won't miss me when I'm not around."

Laying it all out there, making myself say the words, was strangely cathartic in and of itself. The tightness in my chest eased up a bit.

"Oh. Yah, I see." Her eyes turned sad. "I have had boyfriend where . . ." She stopped to think about her words. "Where I like him more."

"Exactly. I had a boyfriend like that, and when we broke up, it was awful, even though I knew he was never going to like me as much as I liked him." I gave a heavy sigh. "And I'm worried—"

"This will happen again," she finished. "That is scary, yah? But . . . I see in his eyes. He watches you when you do not see. Many times, I have seen this."

Really?

My skepticism must have come across in my expression, because she continued, "My boyfriend, he is at home. We did not begin to date for a while. He . . . needed to have time to figure out his feelings." She laughed. "But me, I was knowing from day one."

"So what did you do? How did you two end up together?"

A loud voice called out that the sprint was starting. We turned toward the track and saw the row of guys lined up. Their faces were stern and focused as they bounced on their heels, then lowered themselves into sprint position.

The shot fired, and they took off to the yells of the crowd.

When a tall, thin guy with fiery red hair crossed the finish line, we broke out into whistling applause. His cheeks were stained red, his huge smile practically splitting his face in two.

The next round of runners began to warm up, and we resumed our conversation.

"So, I tell him how I feel and I ask him to his face, do you like me? Because I want to be your girlfriend."

A laugh of surprise barked out of me. "Seriously, you just asked him?"

She shrugged, a bashful grin curving her lips. "And why not? If I know I want to be with him, I should tell him, yah? And not keep it the secret."

Huh. For some reason, I never thought about just outright telling Graham I liked him and I wanted him to stay in contact with me. But maybe I should. Why not? After all, what did I have to lose by being brave? I was a modern girl, and I didn't need to wait around for him to tell me he liked me.

My stomach erupted in a mass of butterflies, and I swallowed. So much easier said than done. Not to mention it was still making myself vulnerable. And if he said no, that he didn't want to stay in touch . . .

"I'm afraid of being rejected," I admitted in a rough whisper.

"It is so scary," she said, empathy clear in her tone. "But . . . when I see him, I see his interest in you. I don't think he will tell you no. I have an older sister. Her name is Sigrid. She is in university in Stockholm, and her boyfriend, he is in university in France. But . . . they have been together for over three years now. If two people want to be together, they will be."

My gaze darted toward Graham again, and I caught him looking at me. His cheeks turned pink, and he looked away, which got my heart racing like crazy.

Maybe Tilda was right. Maybe I'd been missing some big signs just because I was too busy worrying about looking foolish or being rejected. His friend Jamison had told me back in Glasgow that Graham had a crush on me. And we'd done a lot more talking and connecting since then.

Could I really do this? Push aside my fears and just . . . tell him outright that I wanted to stay in touch? If I got too scared to admit my feelings, I could always frame it in the friendship way. Tell him I wanted to keep up to date on his band or something.

But at least I'd be showing interest and putting the ball in his court. And other people have made it work out long distance. Besides, I only had two more years of high school left. After that, I could go anywhere, do anything I wanted. Like take vacations to Scotland.

The thought made me smile.

"Thanks for talking to me, Tilda," I said, and impulsively gave her a hug, which she returned with a warm squeeze. "I shouldn't miss the chance of something good because I'm too afraid to take a risk."

"I am glad I am helping."

The next hour or so went by fast. Our group got food, except for my parents, and I tried a bite of haggis for the first time. And it would also be the last time—I couldn't seem to get past the mental block of what I was eating, so my stomach got a little queasy. Graham wouldn't stop laughing at the faces I made and then finished the haggis for me, giving me the rest of his fish-and-chips.

I accepted them gratefully, and when Tilda gave me a look that said, *See?* I rolled my eyes in a good-natured manner at her.

The next couple of hours were fun and thrilling. Huge, muscle-ripped men in kilts began tossing heavy objects—weights, even smoothly buffed tree trunks (which I learned were the infamous cabers). When a contestant got the caber to flip and land on its end, standing straight up, we roared our approval.

Graham stayed close to my side, and though we didn't talk much, the air between us was comfortable and easy. The three of us had a great time, and by the time the bagpipes and drums band came on the field to signal the end of the games, I was tired, a little sunburned, but very, very happy.

The bus ride back to our B and B was hushed. I mulled over Tilda's words. She was right. If I wanted it, I should just ask for it. Maybe even tomorrow. Determination and courage filled me. I grabbed my earbuds, popped them into my phone, and turned on music to help me unwind.

Chapter ✎ Thirteen

arly the next morning, I wanted to send a message to Corinne, since I hadn't talked to her in a while. Dad opened his computer and let me access the chat messenger. He left to probably go grab coffee, and I settled in at the tiny wooden desk in our room.

I didn't have a separate bedroom this time, but the room was so charming, I didn't mind. The wallpaper was blue-striped, and our beds were cozy with several blankets layered on. I'd slept hard and woken up refreshed.

When I got on the messenger, I saw something from Corinne, and my heart thrilled.

> **FoxyCori: Hey, you! I know you're in bed, dreaming about cute Scottish guys. Hope you're having fun!**

Miss you like crazy. XO. *So* much to catch up on
when you get home.

I could hardly believe this was my ninth day in Scotland. Just four full days left in our bus tour, then a last day in Edinburgh before going home. Time was flying by a little too fast, even though I missed Corinne and couldn't wait to talk to her. I typed out my reply:

AvaBee: Scotland is amazing so far. Check out
these pics. Yesterday we went to the Inverness
Highland Games!

I uploaded shots of the kilted men throwing cabers, the dancers, the haggis I hadn't finished. Then I did one of our entire group, which a kind stranger had taken for us with my camera.

AvaBee: Today we're going to a battlefield and then
touring a glen. This country is so beautiful. I wish
my pictures captured it better.
AvaBee: Okay, signing off. XO can't wait to catch up
with you!

I logged out, got dressed, and popped down the hall to meet my parents for breakfast. This dining room had one long table—it was a smaller inn than where we'd stayed in Oban, but the owner was a friendly man around my parents' age who was attentive and ran a tight ship.

We ate quickly, then made our way to the bus. I noticed the German family was missing the mom and one of the boys.

"Is everything okay with them?" I asked my mom with a nod in their direction.

"Steaphan said the other little boy wasn't feeling well, so his mom is staying here with him for the day."

"Oh, that's a bummer. You've been doing okay, right? No more migraines?"

She beamed at me and stroked my hair. "I'm fine, honey. Sometimes I get those random flare-ups, but I've been careful to avoid triggers. Ready to do more exploring today?"

I nodded, and we got on the bus. Graham was already there, his eyes warm and inviting when they hit mine.

"Mornin', Ava," he said in that husky, familiar way of his.

My chest tightened, and it took me a moment before I could reply. "Good morning, Graham. I'm looking forward to today's trip."

He nodded. "We'll be leaving in a few minutes. My da is just making sure Lucas is taken care of before we go. Poor lad."

I leaned on the seat opposite his, still standing in the aisle. Everyone else except Steaphan was on the bus, so I wasn't going to block anyone from entering. "Yeah, I heard he's not feeling well."

"He woke up with a stomachache."

I remembered Lucas shoveling in multiple handfuls of candy

and sweets yesterday at the Highland Games. Apparently, Graham remembered it too, because he chuckled with me.

"Aye, not so surprised about that, are we?"

"I can't blame the kid. When I was that age, getting to eat that much junk food was worth the cost of stomach pains."

His dad finally boarded the bus and gave me a wink. "Mornin', Ava! Okay, group. We're leaving in just a minute. Find yer seats, please."

I waved my fingers at Graham, then at Tilda when I passed her row, and she grinned. Then I got to my seat and tucked into the corner.

The ride to the battlefield passed in a blur of scenery outside that was over before I realized it. So much green and grass and trees and nature. It made my soul feel at peace. I could easily see why Graham liked doing the tours with his dad. What a great chance to explore your own countryside, and relax, too!

The bus pulled to a stop, and Steaphan stood and faced us. His face was serious, an unusual look for him, and the general hum of our group went silent.

"I just wanted to remind ya that this is a war grave. The brutal, bloody Battle of Culloden was fought here, and many brave Scottish warriors fell and were buried in this land while defending our country. They say around twelve hundred people died in just one hour. Please be respectful—no yelling, no running. As we stroll the battlegrounds, look for the stone grave markers that tell which clan members were buried here. We'll stay here for a bit, then go to one of the loveliest glens you'll ever see in yer life. After that, free time back in Inverness."

We nodded in response and followed him off the bus. The wind had picked up and blew briskly across the massive expanse of field, rippling the tall grasses. Nearby was a modern-looking building with cool arched roofs. Several clusters of people strolled the grounds here and there, and there was a respectful tone of silence throughout.

"After our tour through the battlefield, there's the visitor center if anyone would like to check it out," Steaphan continued when we were gathered in a semicircle around him. "Or you may roam the field at your leisure. Please be back at the bus at eleven. We'll eat at the glen—trust me, it's worth the wait."

Steaphan waved us on toward the start of our battlefield tour, and our group listened intently as he led us through the high heather and shrub-spotted grounds. He explained the background of the battle and the outcome, how the Scottish and Gaelic culture had been altered through the subsequent suppression of their way of life. Clans were impacted because of having their powers stripped. Even tartan wearing had been banned except for those in the military.

I could see stone markers poking up along a strip of old road running through the battlefield, etched with the names of fallen clans, and my heart tightened in my chest. What a tragedy. This reminded me of the same haunted feeling I'd had in Gettysburg. The sensation of thousands of battle cries echoing across the fields.

The brutal result of that fight and how it changed the landscape of the country for good.

We came upon a stone circular building about twenty feet high with a memorial marker set in the bottom, honoring those who fought in the battle in 1746. I took a photo of it and noted a small bundle of flowers beside it.

"This is called a memorial cairn," Graham explained to us. "It was built in the late 1800s, at the same time those memorial markers along the road were installed." He then pointed toward a charming thatched-roof farmhouse. "That building dates to the late 1800s and is on the location where they think a field hospital stood."

His eyes locked on mine, and a small shiver ran through me. He was so intense, unlike most of the guys I knew at home. He was proud of his knowledge of history, didn't try to dumb himself down. That self-confidence drew me like a beacon.

After a moment of silence, Graham looked away from me, and I swallowed. Crammed my hands in my pockets. Peered around the field to see the tall yellow grasses swaying. The hills rolled gently. Yes, this was a place of sadness and grief, yet like Scotland itself, the land had healed and moved forward. Still proud, still noble, even after defeat.

Steaphan and Graham finished talking, and Steaphan invited us all to tour around the battlegrounds on our own. Graham took a step toward me, but the German dad flagged him down and began peppering him with questions. He shot an apologetic smile at me, and I waved at him not to worry about it. After all, he was just doing his job.

So I strolled the grounds with my parents, and we compared the experience to Gettysburg. They felt the same as I did—the heaviness of memory lingering in the air, mingled with the modern determination to keep on keeping on.

When time was up, we got back to the bus and rode in silence for the most part to our next destination. There were a few whispers here and there, but I think we were all still sobered by the powerful experience of the battlefield.

It took us a while to get to the glen. But finally the bus stopped, and Graham stood to address us. His eyes almost caressed me for a few seconds, and then he glanced at the rest of the group. "We're here at Glen Affric. We've packed a lunch to eat in the glen, so I hope yer hungry. It seems the weather has held up, so we can have it outside."

The German dad whispered to his son Karl, who cried out, "*Ja! Ja!*" with fierce nods, and we all laughed. Frankly, I was starving too.

Lunch consisted of sandwiches on thick, crusty bread with an assortment of cheese, crackers, fruit, cookies, and all kinds of drinks. Graham, Tilda, and I carried the food-laden bags up the crest of a hill and found a flat clearing that offered one of the most stunning views I'd ever seen in my life.

Water ran in a lazy river through the grounds below, occasionally speckled with small clusters of scrubby brush, and the sunlight dappled across the rich expanse of green grasses. There were numerous green-coated hills and mountains, as far as the eye could see, with several tops piercing a few low-lying clouds. It was almost unreal, the scene was so idyllic.

I stopped in my tracks and just . . . stared. My breath had locked in my lungs from shock at the view. Miles and miles of sheer beauty right before me.

"This is it," Graham said in a low whisper right beside me. He was so close his mouth had to be just an inch or so from my ear, and goose bumps broke out across my skin in reaction to his proximity. "The place I was eager to show ya."

"I can see why," I replied in a rush. "It's . . . just phenomenal. I can't wait to finish eating so I can explore." I wanted to photograph everything, to draw everything. My brain scrambled to capture the various shades of green and brown and blue and yellow. So much in front of me.

We laid down several blankets, courtesy of Steaphan, and everyone got food and began to eat. My sandwich was so good I took an extra one, and Tilda, seated beside me, threw me a wide grin.

I shrugged with a chuckle. "I'm a growing girl." I'd never been ashamed of my healthy appetite.

Her grin grew wider, and she grabbed another sandwich too. "And I am growing as well."

After we ate, I grabbed a pen from my backpack and a fresh piece of paper and asked for all of Tilda's contact information so we could connect when I got back home. I really liked this girl and had enjoyed getting to know her so far.

Her face flushed in pleasure, and she wrote her address, e-mail, and social media information for me, then asked for the same in return.

"So . . ." She paused and seemed to think about her words. "Have you asked him yet about talking? When you are returning to America, that is?"

I swallowed as a fresh bout of nerves swept over me. "I've just been waiting for the right moment. Probably in another day or two, once we get closer to our time being over."

"He will be saying yes," she replied, certainty clear in her voice. "I know this."

We cleaned up our trash and packed it back in the bag, and then I crammed that into the corner of my backpack. Around us, the others were doing the same as they finished their lunches.

Tilda's mom waved at her, a friendly smile on her face.

"Oh, I promise my parents I will walk with them. We talk more later?"

I nodded. "Absolutely. Okay, have fun!" She headed toward them, and I saw my parents were sitting side by side on their blanket, oblivious to anything around them. Not wanting to disturb their romantic bubble, I made sure I was within viewing distance, then dug out my camera and began snapping shots. This would be another place to get a fun panoramic picture collage done.

I heard the click of a photo being taken behind me and turned

around. It was Graham. And the camera was aimed right at . . .
me. My heart stuttered a beat or two, then began a furious gallop.

He started walking toward me and put the camera down, an
unusually open look in his eyes. I put my camera back in the bag
and flung the strap over my shoulder.

"Why did you take a picture of me?" I asked him.

He gave a casual shrug, but the look on his face was anything
but easygoing. In fact, intensity like I'd never seen poured from his
eyes into mine. "This is my favorite scenic spot in all of Scotland. I
wanted a photo of you here."

My breath caught in my throat, and all I could do was stare
at him. I could feel myself melting into a little puddle right here
in the glen.

He moved closer until he was just inches from me again, and
that crackling electricity rolled between us. There might as well
have been no one else in the glen right now, because we only had
eyes for each other.

Pulse hammering, I scrambled for something to say. "I can see
why you love this place."

He nodded. "Once you're here, you understand."

"It's like a dream, a fantasy," I gushed enthusiastically. "Almost
unreal, in a way. So different from anything I've ever experienced
in America. I'm glad I got pictures of this, but I already know I'm
never going to forget my time here. Thank you so much for being
a part of that."

He blinked, and something seemed to drop between us, a kind

of wall. His jaw ticked as he stood in silence for a moment. "Aye. I see."

My chest lurched. "You see what?" Had I said something wrong? I'd just been complimenting his country and gushing about how beautiful it was.

Graham stepped back from me and exhaled. His eyes were shuttered now, unemotional. He stared at the glen. There was a disdainful scoff in his voice as he said, "You American girls, you always say the same thing."

With a throat suddenly so tight I couldn't speak, I spun around and left. My mind struggled to understand what had changed things between us like that. No way was I going to let him see the tears of hurt and confusion that had flown to my eyes with that dismissive comment, though.

I tugged my camera bag higher up my shoulder as I walked. Chin high, I swept the tears from my eyes, then gave a broad, fake smile to my parents and asked if they wanted to go on a hike. I needed to get away from him, give myself time to process this unwanted feeling of being totally lumped in with everyone else.

Stupid me. I'd thought Graham saw me as special and different, that he was as drawn to my uniqueness as I was to his. But he made it sound like I was nothing more than another shallow, cookie-cutter American girl to him. Unmemorable.

Just one in a line of girls he'd quickly forget as soon as I went home.

And the realization cut me right through the heart.

Chapter ✦ Fourteen

The bus ride on Sunday morning for our day trip in Pitlochry went smoothly. We arrived in just under two hours, and everyone spilled off the bus. I waited for it to completely empty out before exiting and then darted right over to my parents' side.

I could sense Graham's eyes on me, but I didn't look at him. I couldn't. I knew he'd see the emotions clear on my face. The harsh reminder I'd gotten yesterday about being nothing more than a paying customer, a generic *American* tourist, had resonated with me all afternoon and evening. I'd been avoiding him since the glen and had spent my time with Tilda or my parents.

Last night in bed, I'd stared at the ceiling in the dark, wondering what had gone so wrong. The only thing I could think of was that American girl he'd mentioned from last year; I must have reminded him of her somehow.

Still, that didn't excuse him for being so . . . cold. So dismissive, like I was just a random, nameless person who didn't matter. After all these days getting to know each other, I thought we'd become closer than that.

It hurt to know I was wrong.

I stuffed my emotional soreness back in my chest and turned my face to smile at my parents. Whatever. Counting today, we still had three full days of this bus tour, and I wasn't going to let some guy ruin it for me.

Even as I thought that, I knew he wasn't just *some* guy. That was just my embarrassment and pride speaking.

Steaphan gathered us in our usual semicircle. Graham was by his side and whispered something to Tilda, who stood to Graham's other side. Sunlight shone on their faces. I hadn't told her what had happened between me and him, not wanting to dump my woes on anyone else right now.

People filtered by us, giving our group welcoming smiles and waves. It was pretty obvious we were tourists, given that we were right by a tour bus, but like everywhere we'd been, the locals were friendly and kind.

"Welcome to Pitlochry!" Steaphan said with a giddy grin as he spread his arms wide. We were currently parked just off a main street filled with bright, perky buildings and bustling local businesses. "I love this wee town. It's fun and has a lot to offer visitors. There's shopping, art galleries, beautiful gardens, plenty of places to hike, and more. Oh, and don't forget the golfing. Speaking of, I'll unlock the bus storage so we can get yer clubs out." He gave my parents a wink.

Ah, crud. They were golfing again—how had I missed that? Oh, right—because I'd run out of breakfast right onto the bus, and then put my face in a book to avoid having to see or talk to Graham. I hadn't seen my parents pack their clubs back in our room. Nor had I heard much of anything else this morning; I'd been too stuck in my own head.

But as I thought on it, I remembered Mom mentioning at the beginning of the bus tour that she and Dad were going to golf in Pitlochry, and I could rent clubs and play too. At the time I'd agreed, even though I wasn't a golf fan.

Right now, though, I wasn't feeling it. Maybe I could talk her into letting me hang out with Tilda instead, and we could explore those galleries or the gardens.

"Meet back here at eight, please," Steaphan told us all. "No later than that, because we're driving to Inverness, and it's a long, *long* walk back."

The adults chuckled. Tilda's eyes met mine, and we both rolled them good-naturedly. Steaphan was a great guy filled with lots of knowledge about his homeland, but he could be a little corny sometimes.

"Now, off with ya!" Steaphan shooed us all away. "Enjoy

this bonny day. It's supposed to stay sunny and warm."

Mom and Dad got their bags and tucked the straps over their shoulders. "Okay, let's head to the course," she said to both of us.

I drew in a breath. "Um . . . would you mind if I stayed around town instead while you guys golfed? And we can meet up afterward for lunch or something? I just . . . don't feel in the mood for it today."

Mom frowned and eyed my face. "You okay? You have seemed a bit off since yesterday. What's wrong?"

I waved away her concern with the biggest smile I could muster. "Oh, I'm fine. I promise. I just don't really feel up to golfing. I'd rather explore the town instead. I'll see if Tilda can hang out with me so I'm not alone. And I have my phone, and Steaphan is staying in town too, so—"

Mom laughed and held up her hands. "Whoa, slow down. First off, I think your friend Tilda is with her parents today—they're already heading down the street." She nodded past my shoulder, and I looked. Sure enough, Tilda was talking rapidly with her parents as they headed to a cute clothing store.

Well, there went that plan.

Dad shook his head. "I'm not comfortable with you hanging around here by yourself, princess. Sorry."

My stomach sank. I couldn't fault them for wanting to make sure I was safe. "I guess I can just walk around with you guys, even if I don't play."

My face must have been miserable, because my mom just

laughed. "Well, don't flatter us so much into thinking you want to hang with us, Ava."

"I'm sorry." I gave her a hug of apology and let the sincerity show in my eyes. "It's not you, I swear. I just find golf *so* boring." I sighed.

Mom pursed her lips. "Okay. Here's the deal. Since Steaphan will be in town, I'll let you stay here." My hopes soared, only to sink when she continued, "But only if Graham is with you."

Well, there went that. I shook my head.

Mom's brow furrowed. She leaned toward me. "Everything okay? I thought you'd jump at the chance to spend more time with him."

I bit my lip, then said, "I don't know what he's up to anyway. He might be busy with his own plans."

"Graham's not busy at all," Steaphan said from behind us, clapping a hand on my shoulder. "I'm sure he'd be happy to escort ya around town. That's his job."

The reminder only served to rub a bit of salt in my wound. But I gave him an appreciative smile I hoped looked sincere. "That's very nice of you to volunteer him, but—"

"I insist. We pride ourselves on meeting all customer needs, and Graham loves Pitlochry. He'd be thrilled to show ya the sights." Steaphan squeezed my shoulder, then released it. "I'll be back in a moment with him."

My body was one big line of tension as I stood there awkwardly for a moment, struggling with how to fix this mess. Well, when he arrived, I'd simply tell him the services weren't needed.

And then he was right there, peering down at me, and I saw a number of emotions sweeping through his gaze, hard and intense. He turned to look at my parents. "I'm happy to show Ava the gardens." His voice reflected sincerity, tinged with something more resonant.

"It's really okay," I told him in a quiet whisper as I shook my head. "You don't have to do this."

He locked eyes with me again, and this time I could see remorse in them. "I want to. We need to talk."

Obviously he wanted to discuss what had happened yesterday, but I wasn't sure I was ready to hear. Still, I didn't want to be a total jerk, so I gave a quick nod of agreement.

Mom and Dad gave him a grateful look, and then Dad crammed some money in my hand. "Here. Go have fun, princess. We'll plan to meet you in a few hours, okay?"

I watched them walk away and stood there for another awkward moment before finally saying, "Well, let's head to the gardens then."

We made it to the entrance in no time, and I paid for our tickets. Graham had protested, but I reminded him he'd bought my castle ticket in Loch Ness, so we were even now. Rather than easing this tension between us, my words seemed to make it stronger. Maybe because like me, he was remembering how fun and effortless that day had been.

As opposed to today, which was stilted and uncomfortable.

"Erm." He cleared his throat, and we walked in. "So, the garden is divided into different regions, each reflecting a part of the world where Scottish explorers found unique plants and seeds to bring back here."

The gardens were a bit beyond their ideal June bloom, but they were still stunning with their lush richness. There were multicolored plants everywhere that I hadn't seen before. I let their warm summer beauty move me out of my uneasiness into that place where art tapped my soul, opened my eyes. Petals of all shapes and shades, green fronds and leaves and trees pushed against the edges of the path.

We walked in silence for a few minutes, just looking around.

"Ava," he finally said in a low, fervent tone as he touched my arm and drew me to a stop. He pulled me to the side and looked at me, and I could see shadows of regret on his face. "I'm sorry. I feel . . . so terrible. Because what I said came out wrong, and I just want to explain—"

"It's fine," I interrupted, then stopped. I'd told myself I was going to let him explain it if he wanted to. I could give him that courtesy at least. Maybe show him not all American girls were whatever he thought we were. "I'm sorry, please continue. I didn't mean to cut you off."

He reached over and took my hand in his, and my heart thrummed in response to the soft, cautious touch. Everything about him right now was careful, tense, nervous. His back was hunched over, and his eyes looked a little tired.

"Can we sit for a moment, please?" he asked as he nodded toward a nearby empty bench, cast in light from the bright morning sun.

We made our way there and sat down, and he still didn't release my hand, keeping it captured in his.

Graham took in a deep breath, and his hand seemed to shake just a bit, which made my heart soften and wobble. "Ava, I . . . That was so unfair of me to say. I've been kicking myself for it because it was wrong, and I overreacted." His Adam's apple bobbed as he swallowed. "As I mentioned before, an American girl had done our Highland bus tour last year."

Oh. I'd suspected as much—that the girl had been involved in this somehow. Seeing the lingering edge of sadness in his eyes made my heart hurt for him. Obviously she'd caused him pain. He hadn't wanted to talk about any of this back in Oban, yet he was opening up to me now.

Why?

"She lived in California and was here with her family on holiday," he continued. "We spent a lot of time together, and she seemed enchanted with Scotland. With me."

My heart felt a small pang of jealousy, and it was hard to push it back. "Go on," I encouraged him.

He pursed his lips for a moment, then exhaled in a loud huff. "We got to know each other over those days, and she kept talking about what a dream Scotland was, how it wasn't even real."

Ah, now it was all clear. "Obviously this didn't end well," I said.

He shook his head. "She left, and I was broken up about it. But she'd told me she was online. So I found her a week or so after she returned home. Along with a post-Scotland picture of her kissing her boyfriend, some handsome older lad."

"Oh, I'm sorry. That had to hurt a lot." I couldn't imagine how angry and pained he'd felt about that.

"I felt stupid, like I was just a holiday boyfriend for her. Took me a while to stop feeling crushed about it."

"Do you still . . ." I couldn't finish my question.

He shook his head. "No, I don't like her anymore, if that's what yer askin'." He seemed to shake off that shadow, then looked at me and squeezed my hands. "But yer words, they triggered that emotion, and I was afraid. . . ."

"No, I totally get it. I can see how that made you remember what had happened." I looked down at our hands, fingers threaded together, his larger fingers woven through mine. It looked right. It felt right. And my chest ached for this guy who was so generous and kind and had been hurt by someone who had used him.

I was filled with fresh anger about her. I looked up at him. "We're not all like that, you know."

"Aye, I do." Regret poured from his blue eyes. "And I'm so sorry I said that."

"It's okay." I sucked in a breath through my nostrils and then explained a bit about my own personal heartache, how my ex had crushed my heart. As I talked, I could see his jaw tighten in sympathetic anger for me, which warmed my chest.

"It's hard when ya like someone more than the person likes ya back," he said.

"Yes, it is."

Silence stretched between us. The negativity was banished now, our honesty having dispelled it. We were back to where we'd been before. No, that wasn't quite right. A new element had started swelling between us, one brought about because of our pasts.

Sharing those things that made us vulnerable had brought us closer. I could tell he felt the same from the way he sat right beside me, his thigh pressed to my thigh, fingers strong and firm as they held mine.

Graham reached a hand up and tucked a stray strand of my hair behind my ear. His eyes hummed with a warmth that made my skin sizzle in response, and his finger brushed the side of my face. "Thanks for listenin'," he said. "Ya didn't have to, and I appreciate it."

"I'm glad you told me," I replied. "I do understand."

He stood and tugged me with him. His mouth was just inches from mine, and his eyes grew dark. Then he cleared his throat and moved back a fraction. "Ready to see more of the gardens?"

"Definitely."

We walked through the rest of the gardens, our fingers still intertwined, and my heart throbbed with the painful knowledge that I didn't ever want to let go of his hand. Graham had wormed his way into my heart—and all I could think about was proving to him I was the American girl he should risk his own heart on.

Chapter ● Fifteen

The rest of Sunday passed in a blur of activity. After exploring more of Pitlochry, then returning to Inverness, Graham and I sat up late into the evening drinking tea and talking in the lobby of the B and B.

Nestled in a cozy corner beside a small fireplace, the moonlight slanting through the window and candles scattered across the table, we talked about everything under the sun—what movies we thought were funniest, our views on politics, even our pets. Graham said he had a fluffy white dog at home his mom spoiled like crazy, and I talked about my cat.

He laughed when he saw the picture on my phone of my cat wrapped around my head. It was her favorite sleeping position, and most mornings I woke up that way, sweaty and covered in cat hair. I missed the little furball, but I knew my aunt and uncle were taking good care of her.

Monday morning we packed our belongings and drove toward St. Andrews, the final city in our weeklong bus tour. On our way to St. Andrews, we stopped to visit the massive, imposing Glamis Castle, which was supposedly haunted. While it was eerie and old, I didn't find any ghosts, though Graham thought it was funny to grab my waist at one point in the tour and scare me to death. Tilda laughed so hard she snorted, and I elbowed her and made her wheeze.

After exploring the castle, we checked out Meigle Museum to see ancient carved stones and fragments, ate dinner in a small family-owned restaurant near our B and B, and went to bed early. It had been a busy day, and we were all glad to head upstairs to our rooms to relax.

Naturally, the same as every night now, I found myself falling asleep with thoughts of Graham on my mind. That shock of black hair, those blue eyes that made me want to fall into them.

The guy had nestled himself into every crack and corner of my brain.

Of my heart.

When I woke up on Tuesday after taking far too long to fall asleep the night before, I was a little tired but determined to push my fatigue aside. After all, it was the last full day of our bus tour. Tomorrow our family would venture back to Edinburgh, and then start the long flight back home.

Away from Scotland.

Away from *him*.

My stomach was a total mess of nerves, but I made myself go to breakfast and eat a biscuit with honey and a cup of tea. The B and B owner had several cans of soda, so I chugged one to help fuel me with energy, despite my mom's raised eyebrow. I needed the caffeine buzz to jump-start my brain; at some point today, I was going to figure out the perfect way to admit to Graham that I liked him and ask if we could stay in touch.

The thought made my hands shake, so I dropped them into my lap and pressed them together. My palms were already clammy, and I hadn't even done anything yet. I told myself that it was all going to be fine. He'd taken the time to open up to me about his fears, so reaching out to him should assuage them. I would be showing initiative, not making Graham worry that I was just interested in him while we were here.

No, it was far, far more than that.

We stepped onto the bus, and my chest got a little tight as a swell of sadness hit me. I looked over the plush seats, the comfy interior, our home away from home for the last week. I couldn't believe the trip was almost over. It was going to be so hard not seeing Graham every day in person. I'd been unbelievably lucky to spend this much time with him, and the memories of this trip would have to do for now.

If he liked me too, if he wanted to stay in touch with me after

I left, we'd work things out. It was my mantra, one I kept repeating to myself to help bolster my courage.

I took my seat and waved at the two little kids, who waved back, then resumed their rapid-fire chatting with each other. They didn't talk much to anyone else but their parents or Graham—for some reason, they really were attached to him—but they were generally in good moods and had friendly dispositions.

Tilda boarded the bus next and beamed at me as she took the spot beside her parents.

Graham got on after, followed by my parents and Steaphan, and then Graham closed the door and propped his hands on the metal bar beside his seat.

"Gooooood mornin'!" Steaphan called out in his usual jovial tone. He was probably the happiest man I'd ever met.

We all repeated the greeting back to him in a singsong tone.

Graham's warm gaze slid to mine, and my throat tightened as the full impact of leaving him socked me square in the heart right then.

I was going to have to say good-bye to him far too soon. It was so unfair.

Steaphan started talking to our group about today's adventures in St. Andrews, starting with exploring the ruins of the medieval cathedral, but I couldn't focus on his words. A small flutter of emotion built in my chest, and I blinked back the burning tears that threatened to burst from my eyes.

I turned my gaze down to my lap as I struggled to get my emotions under control. The last thing I wanted to do was let anyone discover me like this. Especially not my folks.

Logically, I knew it was crazy—how could I have become this attached to a guy in, what, a week and a half or so? But the pain in my heart told me that wacky or not, it xwas true. I was falling head over heels for Graham. And I felt cheated out of the chance to spend more in-person time with him, the way I would have if we lived closer to each other.

I swept my hands across my eyes to clear my vision and made myself focus on the positives. If I'd never come to Scotland, I'd never have met him. I'd have gone through my life without ever seeing his smile, feeling his hand wrapped in mine. That in itself was something good to remember.

Funny how Graham had started to change me, even in this short amount of time. I was way more interested in history than I ever used to be, and I planned to learn more about my own country, my own state when I got home. I'd become a bit more courageous, more honest—in the last few days, I'd told Graham things I hadn't even told my best friend, like the truth about my ex, or about my childish fantasies about fairies and unicorns. Corinne would have given me the side eye for being weird, since she was such a pragmatic person.

But not Graham. He'd opened up and told me about his childhood obsession with Nessie, and on Sunday he'd admitted how he'd hunted down every fairy ring he could find in the hopes of capturing a fairy of his own.

He didn't make me feel goofy or strange. With him, I could be myself.

Surely he felt this too.

The bus started to move, and I dared to look up at him again. He was talking with Tilda, then after a moment stood and strolled down the aisle toward me.

"Everything okay?" he asked in a concerned tone as he sat down, the length of his thigh searing mine. Today he had on a black long-sleeved shirt and faded jeans that accented every lean muscle in his body. The sleeves were pushed up his forearms so I could see the light dusting of hair on them.

I sucked in a deep breath of that soap scent I'd grown so fond of and said, "Oh, yeah, I'm fine, thanks. I just can't believe it's almost over."

His hand dropped to his thigh, then casually slid toward mine. His thumb brushed my fingers, and my flesh awakened from the soft touch. "Me neither," he admitted. "But I'm glad we met, Ava." The light outside was low but strong enough to catch in his eyes, and I couldn't stop staring at him.

"I am too. It's been so much fun." I knew my feelings had to be written all over my face, and at the moment I didn't care. I wanted him to see how much I liked him. How strongly he made me feel. After David, I wasn't sure I'd let myself open up to another guy again, to trust someone. But Graham gave me a reason to.

The bus ride to the cathedral was quick, only a few minutes for us to get to our parking place. We exited the bus, with Graham pressing his hand on my lower back to guide me off. His gentlemanly gestures were so thoughtful and swoon-worthy.

"We'll be travelin' round St. Andrews as a group today," Steaphan reminded us, "so don't wander off." His mock-stern eyes shot to me, Tilda, and Graham, all standing together, and the adults laughed. "Okay, first up is the cathedral. Get yer cameras ready—it's stunning. Ya won't want to miss this photo opportunity."

The parents walked together, and we three teenagers hung slightly behind in unspoken agreement. Since we'd all started bonding, we'd been spending most of our time together.

"No getting lost," Tilda said to me in a quiet tone as she waggled her finger in my face. "Or you are in big trouble, Ava."

I snorted. "Thanks, Mom."

Steaphan paid our way in, and as we approached the cathedral ruins, I stopped in my tracks for a moment and just stared. Unbelievable.

"It's the largest ever built in Scotland," Graham said in a low rumble near my ear. He pressed that hand to my back again to remind me to stay with the group, and I wanted to keep leaning against it. "It dates back to the mid-1100s."

The stones were old, and the tinge of salt water in the air from the nearby St. Andrews Bay made history come alive here. I craned my neck to peer up the facade of the building. We entered the archway and strolled across plush green grass.

Steaphan gave a brief lecture about the history of the cathedral and how its fall came about in the sixteenth century, due to the Scottish Reformation. Since it was a monument now, the ruins were protected and cared for.

Sunlight peeked through small breaks in the clouds. The temperature hovered in the midsixties, and the wind danced from over the water to greet us. I zipped my fleece up just a touch more.

As the rest of our group lingered and wandered around the massive open grounds, Tilda tilted her head and eyed Graham. "You enjoy being a guide, yah?" she asked him.

He beamed, and his teeth flashed white with his broad, earnest grin. "Aye, I do."

"So, do you also enjoy travel? Go on holiday?"

Good question. We hadn't discussed traveling or other vacations yet. I rubbed my fingers along a row of stone and listened.

"I've been to Germany—bonny country." He paused, and his face grew wistful as he thought. "And Spain is enchanting. The food . . . I just wanted to keep eatin'."

Tilda and I chuckled. Then she asked, "You are planning to see America maybe sometime?"

He blinked, and the easiness left his face. My stomach dropped at the sudden change.

"Tilda!" her father called out with a wave, and then issued a string of rapid-fire words in Swedish.

"I must be going to them," she said with an apologetic smile. She reached out and squeezed my forearm. "I am sorry. I mean no harm." Those last words were under her breath and aimed just at me.

"It's okay," I soothed.

She walked off to join them, which left Graham and me alone.

"So—," I started, right as he said, "I just—"

We both paused and gave awkward chuckles.

"Um, go ahead," I said as we continued to walk slowly toward the back of the ruined structure.

"No, no, please," he insisted.

I dragged in a breath, exhaled, then forced myself to say, "I want to keep in touch with you after I get home, Graham."

He blinked twice, then said, "Oh. Um, I . . ." Cleared his throat, and his cheeks tinged pink. "Well . . ."

Oh no, this was so awkward. My heart gave a sick thud, and I waved my hands in a desperate attempt to backpedal. "It's totally up to you, of course," I rushed to say. God, was he going to brush me off, after all? "Sorry. I didn't mean to put pressure—"

"That would be great," he said, interrupting me. "Sorry, I'm so . . . bad at this." He rubbed the back of his neck, and I saw the tension in his stiff spine.

My heart lurched, and I realized that he must just be afraid of getting hurt again. I stretched out my hand and took his free one. "I really like talking to you, Graham. And there's no pressure. I just . . ." I shrugged. "I just want to get to know you more."

He stared at me for what seemed like forever, and I could hear my pulse roaring in my ears. Right now his face was hard to read; I couldn't tell what he was thinking.

Then he released my hand and dug into his pocket, producing a folded piece of paper with a few miscellaneous words jotted on the back. "Have a pen?"

I fumbled through my bag and grabbed a drawing pencil. When he thrust the paper at me, I was careful to write my contact information down as clearly as possible. I included my mailing address, cell phone number, and even e-mail address.

Then I ripped the page in half, handed the sheets to him, and said, "Your turn."

He tucked my information away in his pocket, then his hand flew across the other piece of paper before he returned it to me. I glanced down to see his name and e-mail address, and my chest tightened in excitement.

"Thanks," I whispered.

He nodded, and his smile looked wide and open, but something seemed off between us. What was I missing here? "We should rejoin everyone before da sends out a search party to find us."

I laughed at his attempt to lighten the moment, though I wished I could figure out what had just happened. It was obvious he was conflicted somehow—but why? All the signs pointed to him liking me, even after knowing the truth about my last relationship's failure and what made me nervous.

Graham and I walked to the group and followed along as

Steaphan led us to St. Rule's Tower, and then to the museum, where we saw more artifacts. But our contact info exchange gnawed at the back of my mind.

When we left the cathedral and strolled down the street toward our lunch destination, where Steaphan had made us reservations at a nice pub, it hit me what was worrying me.

I'd given Graham my phone, address, and e-mail. He'd given me e-mail only, despite me providing my info first for him to see.

The realization made my stomach pinch, and I walked in silence down the street, suddenly disheartened. Despite my efforts to shake it off, I couldn't. I knew there was a chance I was reading into this situation and he wasn't giving me a brush-off, as I was afraid.

But that didn't help the voice in the back of my mind that said once I left Scotland, I was probably never going to hear from him again. If he were really into me, wouldn't he have given me more ways to contact him? Like I had for him?

My unease about the whole thing remained the rest of the day.

Chapter ❦ Sixteen

"Home sweet home," Steaphan declared late Wednesday morning as he pulled the bus in front of our hotel in Edinburgh, the one we'd stayed in before. He opened the door to let our family out right at the front entrance.

On our way here, we'd dropped the other two families off at their appropriate places, where they'd take taxis to head to the local airport and fly home. Tilda and I had hugged hard and promised to stay in touch—with her, I could tell it was sincere and that she would. I couldn't wait to find her online and friend her. I already missed her fun sense of humor and her genuine smile.

My parents and I exited the bus for the final time, and Graham helped us get our bags out of the bottom storage. I thanked him in a murmured tone and shouldered my backpack. Then I looked up at the familiar hotel and smiled for a second, glad to spend one last night in Edinburgh. It felt familiar, comforting. Plus, we were going tonight after dinner to pick up our kilts. I was beyond excited to try mine on.

Dad shook Steaphan's hand with lots of enthusiasm. "It's been wonderful. Thank you so much—you've made our trip amazing. And again, I appreciate all the help with research."

Mom nodded and gave Steaphan a hearty hug. "Yes, and tell Mollie I can't wait to see you guys at dinner tonight. It'll be a great way to spend this last evening in Edinburgh."

Graham shot me a sideways look at her words, which I returned with a shaky, polite smile. Ever since the awkward contact info exchange, I'd been on edge because of this guy. Why did he have to be impossible to read? I couldn't tell what he was feeling right now, couldn't discern if he had the same sinking sensation in his chest I did. His face was a smooth mask of politeness.

Then he blinked, and I swore I saw a flicker of something in his eyes, an uncertainty that made him seem vulnerable. "Ava," he started in a hesitant tone, but was interrupted when his dad waved him over. The two of them leaned their heads together as they talked. Then Graham nodded, offered me an apologetic smile, and got on the bus, and I saw him shuffling around inside.

"—going to miss that lad," Steaphan was telling my mom, a bittersweet look on his face as he stared up at the bus windows.

"What do you mean?" she asked him.

I paused in picking up my suitcases and listened to them, not even trying to hide my nosiness.

"Didn't Mollie tell ya?" Steaphan said, sounding surprised. "Graham's moving to America to start school there in the fall."

I froze, unable to hide the small gasp that flew out of my mouth. What had he just said? Was it really true?

"He'll be in Ohio, living with her parents," Graham continued. "Oh, now that I think of it, she was gonna mention it to ya tonight at dinner." He gave an embarrassed chuckle. "Cat's outta the bag now, I suppose."

Mom clapped a hand over her mouth and shot me a brief wide-eyed look, as if she was surprised I hadn't mentioned it to her. Of course, she was assuming I knew about it in the first place. "Oh, that's amazing! But I'm sure it's going to be an adjustment for everyone. And we'll be happy to help out however we can. . . ."

She and Steaphan continued to talk about the upcoming move and his transition to American high school, but I couldn't hear much past the emotions hurtling through me right now. Shock. Anger. Hurt. My stomach was a tight knot, and my fingers shook as they gripped the strap of my backpack.

I struggled to draw in steady breaths.

Wow, talk about being blindsided.

Not once this whole trip had Graham mentioned to me that he was going to move to America. Which seemed like a big, *big* thing to refrain from mentioning in a discussion. As I stood there, staring blindly at the sidewalk, all the pieces fell into place. His hot-and-cold nature toward me, his apparent discomfort at the oddest times while we were talking. How he'd stiffened yesterday in St. Andrews Cathedral when Tilda had asked him about visiting America.

The fact that he'd given me only an e-mail address to reach him, not his home address.

And certainly not his forthcoming American one.

Embarrassment made my cheeks flame, and I white-knuckled my bag strap, jaw clenched painfully tight. It was hard to keep a fake smile on my face when my mouth was wobbling at the corners. This whole time I'd thought he and I had a real chance, but we never did. I was the idiot who hadn't seen it coming.

Once again.

My lungs seized, and I suddenly felt like sobbing. Hot tears burned my eyes, despite my efforts to blink them away. For days I'd been fearing our pending separation, whereas he didn't like me enough to even tell me the truth. I couldn't believe I'd fallen for a guy who cared far less about me than I did him. It was David all over again.

But worse, actually, because Graham knew my vulnerabilities like David never had. We'd shared things with each other that I'd never told anyone else. But to Graham, I was just a dumb American girl, a distraction to kill time during the summer, and the knowledge broke my heart into a thousand pieces.

"Earth to Ava," Mom said, waving her hand in front of her face. Her eyes were wide with concern, and she leaned toward me. Steaphan and Dad were talking now near the front of the bus, and Graham was still inside it, so we were alone. "What's wrong, honey?" she asked me. "You look terrible all of a sudden."

It was hard to make myself speak past a grief-tightened throat. "I'm . . . not feeling well," I finally said. My head throbbed, so it was the truth. At least partially.

She frowned and studied me. I wondered if she suspected the news had been a surprise to me, too—and not the good kind.

I pointed to my head. "Massive headache. Came out of nowhere," I continued, knowing that would get her to stop studying me so closely. I felt bad using her migraines for my deceptive purposes, but there was no way I could talk to anyone about this right now.

I just wanted to lie in bed, cry, and figure out how I was going to scrape together my tattered pride.

Her eyes softened, and she cupped my cheek. "Oh, I'm sorry. Let's get you inside and lying down, okay? I have some medicine you can take if you want to."

We scooped up our bags, and Mom went over to whisper to Dad, then shuffled with me to the front desk. Our check-in was quick, and before I knew it we were in a fresh room, my bed near the windows turned down and inviting me to crawl in.

I dropped my bags, kicked off my shoes, and slid under the covers, still wearing my jeans and shirt, willing myself to hold it all together until Mom left.

"Do you need anything?" she whispered as she went into the bathroom. I heard water running, and she came back out with a wet washcloth and a glass of water.

Her kindness made my heart hurt even more, and for a moment I wanted to just cry in her arms, like I used to when I was little. But I was so mortified at how blind I'd been regarding Graham's interest that I didn't want anyone to know the truth—at least, not yet. Just another secret to pack away deep in my head.

Not to mention we were supposed to have dinner with them tonight. I didn't want to ruin her last night with her friend.

"Thanks," I told her with a watery smile, "but I'll be okay. Go enjoy lunch with Dad."

She rubbed the hair off my brow and kissed my forehead. "Call if you need anything at all. I'll be back to check on you in a couple of hours."

I nodded.

She shut off the light and left me in blissful, dark silence.

I wasn't sure how much time passed as I released the tears I'd been fighting back. I cried for how foolish I felt, how I'd let my guard down. But I also cried because frankly, I was going to miss him, even if it was ridiculous of me to do so. I figured Graham had real reasons for not telling me about his move, and while I didn't know them, I *did* know I hadn't imagined all of our connections. That much I could tell from honest retrospection. He'd held my hand on several occasions. Told me I was pretty. Sought me out time after time during our bus trip.

It was all so confusing and painful to think about. And my poor brain couldn't make any sense of it.

After my tears dried, I sniffled, wiped my face with the wet washcloth, and sat up in bed. I sipped water as I got my rampant emotions under control. No matter what was happening between us, I wasn't going to spend my last day crying in bed. I was in Scotland; when would I ever get this opportunity again?

Grim determination filled me. I checked the time on my phone. Almost eleven thirty a.m. Mom and Dad were probably heading to their lunch reservation right now. Maybe I could text them and tell them I was up and ready to leave the room.

But first . . . Mom had brought Dad's computer in here, and it was currently sitting in its bag on the small desk. I fired it up and logged into chat. It was still early back home, but Corinne might be up if I was lucky. I had a sudden urge just to say hi to her.

> **AvaBee: You awake? I know it's early. . . .**

A pause, then a moment later a message popped up.

> **FoxyCori: OMG!! So glad to hear from you. MISS
> YOU. Woke up a few mins ago and happened to
> hear my messenger chime. Glad I did!**

Fresh tears sprang to my eyes, and in that moment I wanted my best friend's arms wrapped around me. But Corinne didn't know the whole story about Graham—I hadn't even mentioned him to her. So it wouldn't be fair to dump the whole story on her via chat messenger. Not to mention it would take a long time.

No, we could talk about it later, when I got home. In fact, I decided in that moment that I would tell her about David, too. Corinne was sensible; she'd help me sort through this muddle to find the truth.

And I needed to stop hiding the truth from the people who cared about me.

> AvaBee: I miss you too. Sooooo much. We're heading home tmrw.
>
> FoxyCori: It's weird not having you around. Let's have a sleepover soon, k?
>
> AvaBee: Absolutely. I need girl time.
>
> FoxyCori: And you can tell me all about the cute guys you've met.

When in doubt, deflect. My fingers flew across the keys.

> AvaBee: And *you* can tell *me* all about how things are with Matthew. I'm sure I've missed some stuff . . . HINT
>
> FoxyCori: Can you hear me sighing? Lol. Yeah, we have a lot of catching up to do. Have a safe trip home, k? XO
>
> AvaBee: XO. Will holler when I touch down.

I closed messenger, then my dad's computer, and sat there a few minutes. Yeah, I didn't want to sit in this room by myself anymore. I didn't want to be filled with self-pity. I was going to hold my head up high and savor this last day here.

I grabbed my phone and shot Mom a text. *Feeling better. Can I join you for lunch? Where are you?*

The phone buzzed a minute later. *Great! <3 Here's the address— it's on Princes Street, just a few blocks down. Be careful!!* Included was a picture of the building front, plus the address.

I paused, then typed, *It's just you and Dad, right?*

Yup. We're not dining with Mollie and her fam until tonight. Don't worry, I'm sure you look fine. ;-)

She obviously thought I was concerned about Graham seeing me right now, looking like a mess. Well, I kinda was, but not for the reason she thought. It wasn't because I didn't want to look unattractive. It was because I needed time to get my game face on and not have my heart right there on my sleeve. Needed to pretend like this revelation hadn't shaken me so much.

By the time dinner rolled around later, I was going to be the world's greatest actress. He'd never know how much this had hurt my feelings. We could leave after this evening, each going our separate ways, and I'd still have my pride.

I darted into the bathroom and splashed water on my puffy face. I dabbed on a bit of makeup to cover up evidence of crying. Then I smoothed my hair, grabbed my fleece, and left the room. I headed down the hall, trying not to think about Graham and me standing in the rain on the Isle of Iona, or staring at Loch Ness.

Sitting on the bench in Pitlochry as he opened his heart to me.

Oh, this was going to be so, so hard tonight.

As I got outside and turned right, I saw Princes Street Gardens across the street from me on the left. My heart jumped to my throat as more memories bombarded me of lying on the grass right there with Graham.

Who was I kidding? I couldn't escape him. He permeated every corner of Scotland, invaded everything. Right or wrong, I was going to have to accept that and not let it negatively color my memories of this place.

Otherwise, I didn't have a chance in the world of getting over him.

Chapter ✎ Seventeen

collapsed onto my bed and stretched out, arms reaching above me to brush the wallpaper. "I'm exhausted," I declared. My feet throbbed, so I toed off my sneakers and flexed my arches.

Mom laughed. "And it's hasn't even been a full day." She dropped her shopping bags onto the floor in front of her bed and sat down on the edge, legs dangling. "I'm glad you're feeling better, though."

I paused. "Me too. Thanks."

After meeting her and Dad for lunch, the three of us had spent the afternoon enjoying the sights of Edinburgh. Walking and walking and walking, mingled with a bit of shopping. I'd finally found the perfect gift for Corinne—nothing like last-minute. But when I'd seen the silky tartan-patterned scarf wrapped around a mannequin's neck, I knew it was perfect for her.

"I need a coffee," Dad said as he moved away from his computer. "Anyone else want one?"

Mom looked at her watch. "We're heading to dinner soon. Like, in twenty minutes or so."

He shrugged. "Enough time to enjoy a cup."

"I'm good, but thanks," she said with a hearty chuckle. "Have fun breathing in your caffeine rush."

Dad left, and Mom stretched out and rolled onto her side to face me. She propped her head on her hand. "So, Ava. How come you didn't mention to me before that Graham was moving to Ohio?"

I stiffened. Crud, I'd hoped the shopping trip had become enough of a distraction to keep me from having to address the question until later, when I'd had enough time to stop feeling so raw. My brain whirred for something to say that could put a spin on the whole situation and deflect the heat away from my feelings.

Then I gave a soft sigh. *Stop that, Ava. You promised you weren't going to do that anymore.*

That spin-doctoring thing was the same tactic I always used— trying to come up with an angle that didn't make me look foolish or embarrass myself. But where had that gotten me so far with the people I cared about? Nowhere. They had no idea how I really felt, since I shut them out repeatedly.

I turned to my side to face her and mimicked her posture. "I didn't know," I admitted in a low voice. That sinking weight in my chest came back. "He never told me. I didn't learn about it until you did."

"Oh." Realization dawned. She grew quiet, and her eyes grew

sad. "I'm so sorry. That had to be a shock, finding out that way. Why do you think he kept it to himself?"

"I have no idea. I thought we'd been connecting during this trip, Mom. But I must have misread him." It was hard, sharing the truth with her, but to her credit, she didn't push me to keep talking or make me feel bad.

Instead she got up and sat down beside my head, then drew it into her lap and started stroking my hair. The gesture comforted that aching part of my heart, and I sighed and closed my eyes. Just focused on the feel of being nurtured.

"I don't think you misread him, honey," Mom finally said. Her fingers brushed my brow, tucked a strand behind my ear. "I saw the way he looked at you. There was a reason Graham kept those feelings to himself. Are you going to ask him about it? You might want to think about doing so."

My pulse jumped. It was the question I'd been asking myself over and over. Would I confront him, tell him I knew the truth? Or would I sit there tonight at dinner and act like nothing had happened, just wait and see if he'd come to me and tell me about the move?

"I don't know what to do. But a small part of me doesn't want to know why he didn't bother to tell me." As cowardly as it sounded, it was true.

"I understand that. It might help you get some closure, though, if you did ask."

Closure. I knew it was important, but I didn't want closure right then. I wanted to feel like I was worth Graham's honesty.

Worth him taking a risk and dating me when he moved to Ohio. His silence proved I wasn't.

No way to avoid the truth staring me right in the face. He didn't care about me the way I cared about him.

There was a knock on our door.

I rose. "Dad probably forgot his key," I said with a small laugh, then opened it.

Graham stood there, brow furrowed. His eyes looked dark in the dim hallway light. "Ava," he said in that rumble that still impacted me, despite my best efforts.

"Oh. Uh, hello." My chest rose and fell with the effort to maintain my cool composure. I straightened my spine and made myself look him right in the face. "Why are you here?"

"I heard ya weren't feeling well. Everything okay?" The earnestness in his voice confused me, flattered me, yet a twinge of frustration prickled at the back of my mind.

He cared enough about my headache to check on me, but not about the fact that he'd been keeping something huge secret? What was with this guy? Did he even know how he felt about me, about the possibility of us? What game was he playing here?

I deserved better than this back-and-forth stuff. No matter how much my heart was leaping at the nearness of him. I swallowed and pushed that emotion down. Then I made myself resurrect a protective wall around my heart. I couldn't let him hurt me again.

"Hi, Graham," Mom said from behind me. She was seated on the bed, waving at him. "Hon, go ahead and talk in the hall if you want." Her eyes encouraged me strongly to do so. I knew she wanted me to get him to open up about the move.

I gave her a nod of thanks and left the door cracked only a fraction so I wouldn't be locked out. I pressed against the outer edge of the door frame. "I'm fine. Thanks for checking on me," I told him. "Had a headache earlier."

Graham looked strangely vulnerable, his emotions clear in his eyes. Unlike this morning, when I'd been unable to read him at all, I could now see his hesitation, his nervousness. His jaw ticked, and his fingers twitched just slightly at his sides.

Maybe I could do it. Just blurt out that I knew the truth and see what he said.

But that wouldn't satisfy me. I wanted the words to come from him, not because I dragged them out of him. If he couldn't bother to volunteer the info, I wasn't going to beg for it. Right or wrong, I had too much pride.

And I deserved the effort, the chance. It killed me that he didn't seem to agree, but I'd keep reminding myself of my worth until it soothed away my pain.

I thrust my chin in the air. Suddenly I wanted to prove to him I could be happy without him. That he didn't hold my heart in his hands, that I could be strong and independent. Even if I didn't feel it right now.

"In fact, the headache's gone," I told him, "and I had a great time with my parents this afternoon. We went shopping and walked around Edinburgh. It's been a great last day for my trip.

One of the best I've had so far here in Scotland." So not true. But my mouth and my pride wouldn't stop with the story. "I'm looking forward to getting home and seeing my friends again."

I saw the moment his emotions shut down, and he leaned back against the wall opposite me. The way his brow rose, it was apparent he didn't believe me. No doubt I'd poured it on too thick and he saw right through my story. "I see. Well, glad to hear the day went so well for ya."

My heart twisted with guilt over my blatant lie, and I wanted to dig my way out of this hole. But I couldn't open my mouth to tell the truth. All I could think was that it was hypocritical of him to be upset with me, given the way *he'd* lied to *me* by omission.

How tangled this whole thing had gotten. Sorrow swept through me, and I dropped my gaze to the floor to regain the rest of my rapidly fading emotional strength. I just had to get through dinner. Then I wouldn't have to fake this anymore.

And Graham would never know how deeply I was grieving.

Dad walked down the hallway, holding a coffee cup, and stopped when he reached us. His smile faded as he eyed me, then Graham. "Everything okay here?"

"It's fine," I told him in a falsely bright tone as I kept my gaze away from Graham. "We ready to go to dinner?"

My meal smelled delicious, a true Scottish cuisine of grilled salmon, potatoes, and a fresh salad. Too bad my stomach was such a mess that I couldn't seem to enjoy it.

Graham and I sat opposite each other, both in relative silence, as our parents talked and ate, their forks waving in the air to punctuate their running commentary. Thankfully, Graham's move to America wasn't brought up at all, possibly because Mom was doing her best to deflect the general conversation to more adult and neutral topics.

That alone made me glad I'd talked to her about it—she saved the awkward conversation from being forced on us. I made a mental note to hug her for her thoughtfulness when we got back to the room.

Graham nibbled on a slice of bread, and I sipped my water. We each peppered the general conversation with occasional thoughts, so we wouldn't look like total downers. Both of us employing the same social strategies to avoid the tension between us, thick and heavy.

I picked at the remains of my salmon and felt his gaze on me. I didn't dare look up; my heart was ragged from hiding my emotion, and I didn't want to make a scene.

Keep it together a little while longer.

Finally dinner ended, and we exited the restaurant into the cool summer night. The sun was almost on the horizon, and the cloud-scattered sky shone in brilliant shades of blues and pinks.

A beautiful evening.

Our parents walked down the sidewalk, just strolling and talking, and Graham and I were left side by side. I remembered the pressure of his hand in mine just a couple of days ago.

Seemed like longer, given the current circumstances.

His hands were tucked casually in his jacket pocket, and I did the same to avoid the temptation of touching him one last time. Stupid heart didn't seem to realize I was trying my best to protect it from getting even more hurt. Stupid nose dragged in his scent and tried to fix it in my memory. And stupid eyes kept glancing at his profile, the sweep of his lashes, the line of his lips.

I never got that kiss.

"I hope ya have a safe trip home," Graham said, breaking the tense silence between us. "What time do ya head out?"

"Our flight leaves early," I told him. "We go to London and have a layover, then back to New York City and then Ohio." My heart stuttered when I realized he'd soon be making this very flight. On his move to my own state.

Graham would be an hour's drive away from me, but it might as well be Scotland for all it mattered.

Lamplights flickered on as dusk fell. Warm golden light spilled from pubs and stores all along the street, and couples walked arm in arm.

Doubt started to flood my mind. Was I being too stubborn, too self-protective? Even if he didn't want to be with me romantically, I could still be a friend to him in some way. After all, he was moving to a whole new country. That had to be scary. Surely he'd be missing his Scottish home life and might need some help transitioning to American culture.

My heart battered at the invisible wall I'd put up around it. I should give him a chance to explain why he never told me. Maybe I could throw something out there that would invite him to open up. But what could I say that wouldn't sound confrontational?

Or am I making assumptions here? my head retorted. If Graham wanted my help, my friendship, wouldn't he have voluntarily shared info? Wouldn't he want to seek me out?

"You're thinkin' awful hard," Graham murmured. "What's on yer mind?"

I swallowed and paused to find the right words. Peered up at his face and drank in the sight of his features, now so familiar to me. Splashes of darkness cast shadows across his eyes, so I couldn't read them the way I wanted to.

"Just . . . thinking about Scotland," I answered him in a weak voice. I'd chickened out; my pride had kept me from letting myself show him how I felt.

If he wanted to talk to me about his move, he'd had ample time to do so. But he'd chosen to keep it quiet, so I'd respect his wishes and not push myself on him.

Even if it broke my heart to do so.

It was better this way, anyway. And if I kept telling myself that, I'd even start to believe it.

He nodded, and our families stopped at the corner of the street.

"Our van's over here," Mollie said, her voice thick with sadness as she hugged my mom. "I'm going to miss you so much."

Mom hugged her back, and the two friends whispered in each other's ears, tears streaming down their faces. It hurt to watch their grief at parting, and I turned away to give them privacy.

"Thank you for the tour of Scotland," I told Graham past a rapidly tightening throat. I gave myself the luxury of staring at him, implanting his face into my memory. "You helped make this vacation amazing, and I can't thank you enough for it."

He paused and chewed on his lower lip, his brow furrowed. "It was a pleasure meeting ya, Ava."

"You too." Darn tears started filling my eyes, and I looked away and blinked. Gave his parents huge hugs and warm thanks. Finally turned back to him one last time and dared to reach out and take his hand in mine. I couldn't resist the impulse. "Well, then I guess this is good-bye."

His face was a stiff mask, but he clutched my fingers, his hands slightly chilled. "Good-bye."

As he walked away with his parents, I lingered on the corner, watching the tattered pieces of my heart follow him around the bend.

Chapter ● Eighteen

So how was New York?" I asked Corinne with a huge grin as we settled in my bedroom. "I can't wait to hear all about it. You just got home last night, right?" I took her overnight bag and propped it beside my computer desk, where she took a seat in my wheeled chair.

The August heat was just as intense as July's, so I moved to stand over the air-conditioning vent and stuck my face in it. My cheeks were flushed, and a bit of sweat dribbled down my back. Crazy how I still longed for Scotland's more moderate weather.

Hard to believe a month had passed now since I'd been there, wearing fleece and thin sweaters to combat the brisk breezes. Even this tiny tank top felt like too much clothing on.

Corinne sighed with pleasure, and her cheeks had a slight pink tinge. She didn't seem bothered by the heat at all. "It was amazing,

Ava. Not just seeing our painting on the wall of a real live gallery, but . . ." Her dark-brown eyes turned to me, and the uncharacteristic warmth and love I saw radiating from them surprised me. "Matthew and I are together now. We're officially dating." She squealed and popped her hands over her mouth. "Oh my God! He said he loves me, and I just can't get over it all."

I squealed and ran over to give her a hug. "I knew it! I told you it would work out!" A couple of weeks ago, I'd been at Corinne's house spending the night when she'd gotten the call about her and Matthew's painting winning the big art competition. The main prize: a trip to New York City to see their painting displayed in a legit gallery.

At the time, Corinne had been both pleased and crushed, because she and Matthew had had a falling-out. But I'd encouraged her to admit her feelings to him.

Apparently, she had. And it had worked out.

A nervous flutter built in my stomach, and I pulled back from her to sit on the edge of my bed. Corinne had taken my advice to be honest and admit her feelings. Then again, it wasn't a question of Matthew liking her. He'd been open and up-front about that. It was her fear regarding their compatibility that had kept them apart.

Different situation altogether from mine.

Corinne dug into her bag and showed me her copy of the official certificate. Her face shone with pride. "I wish you could have been there with me," she said. "But I wanted to tell you how much

I appreciate and needed your support. I was a total mess, and your advice got me through it. Thank you."

An unexpected burst of tears flew to my eyes. I blinked and waved them away. "I'm so happy for you."

"If you're happy, why do you look so awful? No offense," she said with an apologetic smile. "That came out wrong. But you don't look like yourself, and you haven't since you got home. What's going on?"

It was right on the tip of my tongue to spill the beans to her about Graham. But I didn't want to detract from that glow she had going on. After so much angst and anxiety, Corinne was happy. She deserved it.

"Is this about that guy you met there? We never did finish talking about him, by the way. Somehow we got sidetracked into talking about Matthew instead." I stiffened just a fraction, and her eyes narrowed shrewdly; the girl didn't miss a thing. "Uh-huh. Thought so. Talk."

"Seriously, it's not a big deal."

"You're not one to cry at the drop of a hat."

"I'm just . . . thrilled for you. And it's superhot in here," I replied with dramatic flair as I waved my hand to my face. "Anyone would cry from this heat."

Her face fell, and I could hear the hurt in her words as she said, "We're best friends, Ava. You can tell me anything—but you know that already. God knows you've listened to me talk on and on about Matthew. I just want you to feel like you can do the same."

The soft-spoken words pierced through to my heart. She was right—she'd opened up to me many times, but I wasn't showing her I trusted her enough to do the same . . . despite my promise in Scotland to stop hiding the truth from the people I cared about.

Shame tightened my chest. "I'm sorry," I said in all sincerity. "It's just . . . hard."

She nodded. "I know. Trust me, I get it. Being vulnerable is scary."

I stared at my fumbling fingers for a moment, wondering where to start. My pulse throbbed in my veins, and I wiped away the sweat that had gathered on the sides of my face. "As I told you before, in Scotland, I met a guy."

"The local one with blue eyes," she supplied. "I remember. He was the guy who showed you around."

I nodded. "His name is Graham." I reached down and grabbed the folders of photos Mom had developed last week from the trip. Photos I hadn't dared look at because I knew he was in many of them. My hands trembled, but I made myself open them and pull the images out.

Over the next half hour, I showed the pictures and confessed it all to Corinne, who sat quietly and just listened. I talked about meeting his friends, about the girl in America he'd fallen for, how I'd admitted the truth about David to him—something I hadn't done with Corinne until our conversation post-Scotland.

Her face showed a pinch of hurt when she realized he knew

about it before she did, but she quickly wiped the look off and nodded at me. "Go on."

"Before I do, I need to say I'm sorry." I squeezed her hands. "I've come to realize I have this . . . problem with opening up and letting people see these things that hurt me and make me look foolish."

Her eyes grew deeply sad, and she clenched my hands. "Don't you get it? I'm your best friend. You could never look foolish to me. I'm sorry you felt like I would judge you or something, but I wouldn't. We both know I've screwed up so many times, I have no right to judge anyone." Her wry laugh cracked the edge of tension in the room.

"Thank you. I mean that." I continued my story and told her about the two of us holding hands in the garden, then about exchanging contact information in St. Andrews. My heart began its irregular stutter as it always did when I thought about those last couple of days in Scotland. "I couldn't figure out why he only gave me an e-mail address to contact him. And then I found out the truth. That he was moving to America—Ohio, actually, to live with his mom's parents. I guess he didn't want me to know."

That familiar throb in my chest grew and swelled as Corinne gave a sad little sigh. "Oh, Ava. That had to hurt so badly. I can't imagine how you must have felt."

"I felt stupid. Like all this time, I'd been letting down my guard, letting him into my heart, and it was never meant to be anything other than a little vacation thing." I stared down at the picture of me and Graham standing in front of Loch Ness. The sun glowed on our faces, glinted off my blond hair, highlighted the brilliant blue of his eyes.

Corinne pointed at his face. "That smile is real. This boy wasn't dragging you along. What did he say when you asked him why he never told you?"

I swallowed, and guilt flared anew. "I didn't."

She blinked in surprise. "Wait. So you just got on a plane and left? Did you ever e-mail him after you got home?"

"Why would I?" My voice sounded edgier than I meant, and I tried to lower the defenses that had started rising. "Sorry, I didn't mean to sound so crabby. But he has my contact information too, and I never heard from him."

"And you're too proud to reach out to him and tell him you love him. Oh, Ava. Girl, you're in a mess."

Big tears streamed down my face, and I let that ache I'd been pushing down for a month come out and spill over. "I know," I said with a choked sob. "And over the last month, I can't stop wondering if I was wrong not to reach out to him. After all, he did tell me about that girl he liked who broke his heart. Then again, why only give me an e-mail address? Isn't that a message in itself?"

Corinne got out of the computer chair and sat on the bed beside me. Her hand made soothing circles on my back. "Ever think maybe he was too scared to give you more? I mean, what if he wasn't sure how *you* felt? If he'd given you all his American contact information, what if he never heard from you after the trip, and then he'd put himself all on the line for nothing?"

"But I was supposed to do the same for him? Which I did, actually—and it didn't matter," I said miserably. "Because I haven't heard a word from him, either."

I'd checked my e-mail every hour for days after that trip. There was nothing in there, or on my cell phone, or in the mail, or on my social media. Gradually I stopped looking as much.

A message wasn't ever going to come.

Corinne's laugh wasn't unkind. "Oh wow. I totally see what this is. You're both *so* stubborn. Someone's gonna have to bend if you're gonna make this work. You can't each wait for the other person to be the one to reach out, honey. You know that."

I sniffled and swiped at my tears. "But why does it have to be me? Aren't I worth the effort of someone pursuing me?" My voice broke on that last word, and I swallowed back another sob.

Corinne wrapped me in her arms and stroked my hair. She let me cry for a moment until I started to feel calmer. Then she pulled me away and stared me right in the eyes. "Of course you're worth it. But you haven't given him a chance to pursue you—and your silence doesn't give him any reason to either. It just tells him you're not interested."

I bit my lower lip. Was she right? Once more I mentally scanned through those last couple of days in Scotland. How I'd kept a brave face on and hadn't let him know he'd hurt my feelings.

In fact, I hadn't ever told him I liked him. I'd just assumed he'd figured it out. After all, my feelings were painfully obvious to me, Tilda, my mom, even Jamison.

But what if he hadn't seen it? What if he'd been just as scared as I was, thinking my emotions weren't genuine? And then I'd done exactly what that other American girl had—gone to my home and seemed like I'd forgotten all about him.

I pressed a shaky hand to my mouth. *What have I done?*

"Ava, Graham is not David," Corinne continued. "Don't let yourself get confused and treat him as such. Make sure you're giving him a fair chance before assuming he just meant to use you. You need to talk to him. You need to tell him how you feel. Otherwise, there's no way you guys can work things out."

"What if it's too late? What if he's over it all now?" After all, so much time had passed. Days and days of me slogging through the rest of my summer, trying so hard not to think about Graham so I wouldn't hurt like this. Fat lot of good it did me.

"Do you still feel the same about him?" she asked me plainly.

I nodded. Despite the pain, I couldn't quite let him go.

"I doubt his feelings changed that quickly either. But if they did, he was never the right guy for you in the first place."

"I'm scared," I confessed.

"Trust me. I know. It was the hardest thing in the world for me to tell Matthew how I felt. But the risk is worth the payoff." She smiled at me, and the understanding look helped soothe my aching heart. "If you want someone to risk it all for you, you have to be willing to risk it all for him, too. Don't let him go, honey. Not without at least being honest."

I'd been honest with my mom, with Tilda, with Corinne. But I hadn't been fully honest with him. She was right. How could he know I cared if I never told him?

I nodded, filled with resolve.

"I'm gonna go downstairs and talk to your mom for a bit," Corinne said, then continued before I could protest. "So you'd better sit yourself down at your computer and write this boy an e-mail. Don't hold back. Tell him everything. And I don't want to see you downstairs until you do." She gave me a stern squint and wagged her fingers.

She closed the door behind her, leaving me alone with my hundreds of thoughts. I ran a hand through my hair and sighed.

What should I say? Was I ready to take that risk, a jump in the dark? Was Graham worth it?

I thought about him confessing his Nessie obsession to me. How he loved fairy rings. The passion in his eyes as he talked about history.

The warmth in his hands when he stroked my fingers.

Yes, it was worth the chance.

I opened my e-mail and grabbed the folded scrap of paper I'd abandoned in the corner of my desk. His scrawled handwriting with his name and e-mail address. I started a new message and made myself type all the things in my heart.

Dear Graham,

I'm sure this is a big surprise for you, hearing from me out of nowhere. After all, it's been a while since I left Scotland.

The weather is superhot here. We're in the middle of another heat wave. Lucky us.

But . . . maybe you know this already, huh?

You see, the morning we got back to Edinburgh, I overheard your dad telling my mom that you were moving to Ohio to start school here in the fall. Not sure if it's happened yet or not.

I paused and rubbed my brow against the start of a tension headache. *Courage,* I silently willed myself. My fingers tapped across the keyboard.

We didn't end on the best note, I know. Partly because I was really hurt you never told me you were moving here. My initial reaction was that you didn't like me, that you'd only intended for our connection to be temporary. Just a little vacation friendship or whatever.

So I left Scotland without telling you how I felt. And I regret it. I should have confronted you. I should have told you I knew about the move and asked you why you hadn't said a word the whole trip. But deep down, I was afraid of hearing the truth. Afraid because . . . because I fell for you, and there was a huge chance I was the only one feeling this way. I know that sounds crazy, and it might freak you out, but so be it.

Being with you, being around you, taught me I needed to open up more and be honest. So here it is, the honest truth. Graham, I think you're handsome. You're funny. You're supersmart and talented.

The best part of Scotland, to me, was you.

Fresh tears streaked down my face, but I didn't stop typing to wipe them away. Now that I'd started, I had to keep spilling it all out.

I regret not telling you these things before I left. But I'm so, so glad I met you, because you changed me and made me want to be a better person. I'm also sorry it took me this long to write. Stubborn pride, I guess. I kept waiting for you, but it occurred to me today that maybe you've just been waiting for me, too.

Or . . . maybe not. I really don't know, because you're a hard guy to read sometimes. ;-)

No matter what, I wish you the best of luck in your new home in Ohio, in your new school. If I can ever help you in any way, I hope you'll e-mail me back and let me know. I'm not sending this message to push you into something you don't want. Just to say . . . I miss you. I care about you. And I want you to be happy.

Love,

Ava

My heart was about to slam its way out of my rib cage as I scanned our Loch Ness photo and attached it to my e-mail. I let myself reread the message once to make sure I didn't have any typos.

Then hit send before I could change my mind.

The ball was utterly in Graham's court now. I'd opened myself up to him, and I had no idea what to expect next, if anything.

I closed my computer and darted downstairs before I could let myself freak out about it. "I'm ready for ice cream," I proclaimed as I walked into our kitchen to find Corinne and Mom talking by the counter. "I just earned it."

Corinne gave me a proud grin and squeezed my upper arm. "Yes, you did."

Mom dug into the freezer, grabbed three spoons, and produced a carton of chocolate ice cream. "Ladies, I think this calls for some chocolate."

Chapter ● Nineteen

I sat in the backyard and stretched my legs out on the plush recliner chair. The heat wave had finally broken yesterday, so today was balmy and comfortable. Sunlight poked through leaves in the two tall trees high above my head. A number of birds chirped and sang in the neighbor's yard as they pecked through the grass looking for food.

I sipped my iced tea and scanned my phone's music storage to find a new album to listen to. I selected one and let the mellow music wash over me, adjusted the sound so it was a bit louder in my earbuds, then closed my eyes and sank into the chaise.

Saturday was shaping up to be pretty nice.

A moment later a hand tapped my shoulder. I peeked an eye open to see my mom staring down at me, a strange look on her face. "I need you in the living room, please."

"Okay. Did I forget to finish chores or something?"

"No, you're not in trouble. Just . . . come in here."

The urgency in her voice stirred me into action. I grabbed my tea, tucked my phone and earbuds in my shorts pocket, and followed her through the patio doors into the living room.

Then stopped dead in my tracks, the air whooshed right out of my lungs.

"Afternoon, Ava," Graham said in that lilting rumble I'd missed so much. He had on a pair of shorts and a faded T-shirt, and his black hair looked a touch longer than when I'd last seen it. Beside him were an older couple with friendly smiles—must be his grandparents.

Mom shoved me farther into the living room. "Honey, these are Mollie's parents. We're going to relax and talk for a bit. Will you entertain Graham while we do? I'm sure he doesn't want to sit here and listen to us grown-ups go on and on."

I swallowed and gave a wooden nod, surprise making me temporary incapable of speech.

Graham was here. In my house. He'd come to see me. But why? I hadn't gotten a response to the e-mail I'd sent him several days ago.

Was *this* the response?

"Care for a walk?" he asked me as he stepped close, and I automatically breathed in his scent. It was slightly different. Must be a new soap he was using now.

Since he lived here.

In America.

The full impact of the situation hit me like a smack in the face, and I struggled to get all my runaway emotions under control before I spoke. "Um, yeah. Sure. That would be great. Mom, we'll be back in a bit."

"Take your time," she urged me with a knowing wink. She crammed a few dollar bills in my hand. "Go grab a soda or something if you want."

I slipped into my favorite pair of flip-flops and smoothed the wrinkles out of my dark-blue tank top, since I'd been lying down. Then I opened the front door to wave Graham outside.

The sun was inviting as it caressed my bare limbs. I took a quick peek at his legs—he'd worn jeans the whole time I'd been in Scotland, so I hadn't yet seen those strong calves dusted with dark hair. His legs were lean and fit like the rest of him.

I cleared my throat and said, "Um, so this is my neighborhood." The busy street was lined with pristine, comfortable brick houses, kids laughing and running around, dancing in sprinklers, coloring with chalk on the sidewalk. "Straight ahead there's a major intersection, where we can go find something to drink. If you want, that is."

"Aye, I'd like that." Something about his body language seemed different. Was I seeing him in a new light, or was he more relaxed than he'd been in Scotland? "I got yer message, Ava."

"Oh."

"I wanted to talk in person instead of replyin'. Hope that's all right."

Tension wound around me like a ribbon, and I gave a bobble-head nod. "Sure. Oh, that's totally fine. I mean, I didn't really . . ." Well, to be honest with myself, I hadn't expected a response at all, which was why I was so flabbergasted by his presence.

It was way too tempting to put up the facade and not let him see the way I felt, but I wasn't going to do that anymore. If Graham had come to visit me, he was going to see me as I really was.

We made it to the intersection. I paused and pointed left. "That way leads to Rocky River, and if we keep going right, we'll hit downtown Cleveland."

His lips quirked, and I realized what an odd role reversal we were in. Me playing tour guide to him.

"This is kinda weird," I admitted with an awkward laugh. "I'm sorry."

"Don't apologize." He maintained a polite distance from me, but his eyes seemed like they were saying something I couldn't quite understand.

I wanted to ask him why he was here, what he was thinking, but I'd already done all the confessing so far. If anything else was going to happen, I needed him to be the one to start that discussion. Pride or no, it was important to me.

In the meantime, I scrambled for conversation and guided us to the right, where my favorite coffee shop was just a few blocks away. "So, how are you liking America so far? When did you get in?"

"A coupla weeks ago. Been a strange adjustment, actually. The jet lag was brutal for several days."

"Are you missing home?" My chest ached as I thought about how hard this had to be for him, even if he did want it.

He nodded. "I miss my friends, but we've been talkin' a lot online, and I'm gonna visit home during Christmas. I'll see them then."

"That's good."

Our silence stretched as we walked, and then Graham grabbed my arm and stopped me from walking. I spun around to face him.

"Ava," he whispered, and his hands slid down to cup my shaking fingers. "I missed ya so much."

I bit my lip to fight back the swell of emotion that threatened to burst at his words. "I missed you, too."

He pulled me to stand in the shade of a storefront awning. People strolled by, not paying any attention to us. "I was so wrong and I handled things badly. I was scared because I'd been hurt before."

"I know. It's okay. I understand."

"I don't think ya do." He cupped my cheeks and stared into my eyes, and I didn't breathe for a moment, just absorbed him. "When I met ya, I wanted to tell ya a thousand times that I was moving here. But the timing never seemed right, and it was a lot of pressure to put on us when we'd *just* started talkin'. What if ya'd gotten home and decided ya didn't like me after all? I'd be stuck here with a broken heart, knowing ya were only an hour away."

I swallowed past the knot in my throat. "Oh." It made so much sense now; I'd assumed it was because he didn't care about me.

No, it was because he did—he did, and he was scared to.

His thumbs stroked my cheeks, and then he dropped his hands. Glanced at the ground and drew in a ragged breath. "I've liked ya since the first day I met ya. When I saw ya standin' in front of the castle, so wee and dainty, with yer blond hair glowin' in the sun, I knew I was gonna be a goner. I tried to fight it, but I couldn't."

"Me neither," I whispered. My chest was so swollen with emotion I was sure it would all erupt out of me.

He looked up at me, and I saw the enormity of his emotions at full impact. Graham wasn't hiding anything from me anymore. The honesty on his face took my breath away. "I wanted to e-mail, call, but the way we left each other . . . And then I never got any messages . . . Well, I figured I should leave ya alone. That maybe it *had* been a holiday crush, and that was all." He paused. "Then I got yer e-mail."

I nodded and took a step toward him.

"Did ya mean it? What ya said?"

The uncertainty in his eyes, the nervousness, broke my heart. Just like it had taken courage for me to e-mail him, it took courage for him to face me and make sure this thing between us was genuine.

A tear slipped out the corner of my eye. "Every word," I told him as I took his fingers and wove them with mine. "That wasn't just a vacation fling for me, Graham. I haven't stopped thinking about you since I left. I was scared of getting hurt, but it didn't occur to me at first that maybe you had my same fears. My friend had to point it out."

"So ya talked to someone about me?" That sweet dimple popped out in his cheek.

I smirked and stood until we were touching toe to toe, chest to chest. I craned my neck to peer up at him. "Yes, I did."

"What did ya say?" His voice was low.

I steadied the tremble in my hands and said, "That I fell for this amazing person I was afraid I'd never see again."

"That's funny," he said as he cupped my face again. His eyes grew dark and hooded, and his face inched closer. "Because I told my friends back home the same thing." He brushed his lips across mine, a slight gesture that still made my skin break out in goose bumps. "I'm fallin' for ya, Ava. Will ya be my girlfriend, please?"

Gentlemanly as always. My heart flipped over in response. "Yes. And I'm falling for you, too," I breathed, and then he was kissing me, tasting my mouth, and I was tasting his. I wrapped my arms around him until there weren't any spaces between us, just two souls touching. I'd never felt as close to anyone as I did right now.

His hands slid down to cup my waist, and the heat from our bodies built between us. His mouth explored mine, teasing, drawing me in. I could barely breathe, and I didn't want to.

We heard a wolf whistle behind us and broke apart with a laugh.

Graham scrubbed his hand across his hair, then said with a chuckle, "We should probably head to that coffee shop, eh?"

I nodded. "You'll like this place. They have great scones, too."

His mouth crooked into a lopsided grin, and the impact hit me anew. Oh wow, this gorgeous guy liked me. Was falling for me. Wanted to be with me.

We walked hand in hand to the coffee shop, stepped inside, and breathed in the cool rush of air-conditioning. I spotted a table near the front window, and we sat, scooting our chairs right beside each other.

"I can't believe you're here," I said in a rush. "I feel like I'm dreaming."

His thumb brushed my hand in little circles, and I shivered in response. "It's real, Ava. And I'm ready to make this work with ya."

"Me too. I'm turning sixteen next month, so I'll be able to drive soon." Which meant even more time we could spend together. Graham was the perfect motivator to ace my driver's test. And once he got his license, the sky was the limit on when and where we could meet.

I couldn't wait to introduce him to all my friends. I just knew Corinne would love him.

The smile he gave me melted my insides. I left him there to go order two iced coffees, then brought them to our table and sat down again. He draped an arm over the back of my chair and made lazy swirls with those strong fingers on my shoulder.

I pressed deeper against his side and rested my head on his firm chest. Graham was actually here, with me. It wasn't a dream.

I was so glad I'd taken the risk and e-mailed him. Somehow I knew Corinne would have a smug smile for days over this. I'd be hearing about how right she was—and right now, I couldn't blame her for gloating.

"So," he rumbled, and I looked up to find amusement dancing in his eyes. "As my girlfriend, I'm dependin' on ya to help me become familiar with yer American ways."

I gave a casual shrug. "I suppose I can do that. If . . ."

"If what?"

"If you give me another kiss," I said with a saucy wink. "That's the first rule of having an American girlfriend. You should make sure—"

Graham cut off my goofy speech with a toe-curling kiss, and I sighed with pleasure and threaded my fingers through his hair.

Yeah, a girl could get used to this much happiness.

TURN THE PAGE FOR MORE FLIRTY FUN.

At the Winnie C. Camden Folk School, all the sounds are peaceful and antique—the pling, pling, pling, of hammer dulcimers, the sleepy grind of katydids, the whoosh of fire in forges and kilns. While people are here, whether it's for a weekend workshop or an entire month of quilting or wildflower painting, they will themselves to become antique, too. They pretend they've never heard of Twitter or texting. Somebody always seems to be singing, "Tis the gift to be simple, tis the gift to be free. . ." But me? When I arrived at Camden on the second day of June, my summer barely begun, I made way too much noise. I didn't mean to. (Not entirely, anyway.) But I was driving my grandma's stiff and wheezy van, lumbering from too much cargo. The slightest turn of the steering wheel in the Camden parking lot unleashed a spray of gravel. And when

I'd parked and stumbled out of the driver's seat—stiff and sore after the four-hour journey from Atlanta to North Carolina—I accidentally slammed my door.

At least, I think it was an accident.

Maybe I was just bad with cars. I'd only had my learner's permit for three weeks.

"Please remind me why I agreed to let you drive?" my grandma asked as she creaked out of the passenger seat and shuffled toward the back of the van.

I circled around, too, meeting Nanny by the trunk.

"Because you have an iron stomach and I always get carsick up here?" I offered. Camden lay in a valley blockaded on all sides by mountains. The only way to reach it was along nauseatingly twisty roads.

"Or, maybe," I posed, smiling slyly as I leaned against our van's dented bumper, "you feel terrible for dragging me to no-wifi purgatory for the entire summer."

"Well, let me think on that," Nanny said, tapping a short-nailed fingertip against her pursed lips. "Do I feel bad for bringing you here for four weeks out of your nine-week summer? Do I feel guilty for asking you to assist in my fiddle class after being your one and only music teacher since you were three?"

I squirmed as Nanny moved her finger to her chin and pretended to give these questions serious consideration.

"Do I feel sorry for you," she went on, "because you broke curfew one too many times and your parents sent you here, to one of the most beautiful places on earth, as 'punishment?'"

Nanny made exaggerated air quotes with her fingers.

I folded my arms and sighed. I should have known not to give my grandma that easy opening. Maybe it was being a musician that gave her such perfect pitch for sarcasm. Once she got on a roll, she could improv forever.

Nanny gazed at the sky and mock-contemplated for another beat before she looked at me and grinned.

"Nope, my conscience is clear," she said. "But thank you for your concern, Nellie."

I rolled my eyes, but couldn't stifle a tiny snort as I popped open the trunk door. That was another talent of Nanny's. She could make me laugh even as she was doing something hideously parental like carting me off to folk music jail and calling me "Nellie" instead of Nell.

I started to pull our fiddle cases and bags out of the van, but before I could hand anything to Nanny, she'd set off across the parking lot, stretching her wiry arms over her head.

"What about our stuff?" I called after her.

Still walking, she tossed her answer over her shoulder.

"We'll get 'em after we check in."

There was an eagerness, even a little breathlessness, in her scratchy voice.

I'd almost forgotten that, as full-of-dread as I was about this summer, that's how excited Nanny was. She'd been teaching fiddle classes here for way longer than I'd been alive. Only birth or death kept her from her Camden summers—literally. She'd stayed home the summer that I was born fifteen years ago, and then again when my brother Carl arrived.

Then, when Carl was four and I was nine, my grandfather got sick, very sick. Nanny cancelled her month at Camden once again. A few weeks later, PawPaw died. That's when Camden came to Nanny. In the over air-conditioned funeral home, one of the textile teachers draped Nanny's shoulders in a beautiful, hand-knitted shawl. A couple wood carvers spent a whole night etching gorgeous designs into PawPaw's simple casket. And, oh, the music. The music never stopped.

That helped most of all. Because in our family, music is the constant, the normal. Somebody is always picking or bowing, strumming or singing. On any given day in our house—and in Nanny's down the street—there are recordings happening in the basement and lessons being conducted in the front parlor. Dinner parties don't end with dessert but with front porch jam sessions. Nanny, my parents, and their many musician friends stick to Irish, Appalachian, folk and roots music, anything so long as it's really old. Bonus points if the lyrics involve coal miners with black lung or mothers dying in childbirth.

The strumming, singing, plinking is so constant, I barely hear it anymore. Music is the old framed photos that cover our bungalow walls, our faded rag rugs, and our tarnished, mismatched silverware—treasures to some, wallpaper to me.

Maybe that's why, as I followed Nanny onto the student-crowded lawn in front of the Camden lodge, it took me a moment to realize that somebody was playing a fiddle. It only registered when I saw Nanny veer away from the beeline she'd been making to the lodge. Then I noticed other students milling around the lawn cocking their heads, grinning, and following Nanny to a circle that had gathered around the musician playing the song. The tune was clear, sweet, strong, and of course, very vintage.

From the outskirts of the small crowd that had gathered, I couldn't see the fiddler. I could only glimpse the tip of his or her violin bow bobbing gracefully against the sky. But I didn't mind. I took a step back so I could eye the spectators instead.

Camden was one of those "ages nine to ninety-nine!" kind of places, so I wasn't surprised to see some earth-mamas with long braids trailing down their backs, men in beards and plaid, and grandparent-types wearing sensible sandals and sunhats. A lot of the kids were just that—kids. They looked a lot more like my ten-year-old brother than like me. They were probably here because they dreamed of being Laura Ingalls Wilder or Johnny Tremain. I knew this because the last time I'd come to Camden, as an eleven-year-old, I'd wanted to be Anne of Green Gables.

But soon after that, I'd started to find the Camden school too earnest, too stifling. It was the only place, outside of Santa's workshop, that I associated with the word jolly.

There were clearly plenty of teenagers here who didn't feel

the same way. A few of them were in this group listening to the fiddler. There were two guys with patchy facial hair, wearing serious hiking boots and backpacks elaborately networked with canteens and compasses.

There was also a girl who looked about my age. Her pink cheeks looked freshly scrubbed. Her long, sand-colored hair was plaited into braids that snaked out from beneath a red bandana. She wore black cargo shorts and white clogs.

Since she was engrossed in the violin music, I could stare at her and wonder which class she was taking. She didn't seem like a spinning/knitting type—they always wore flowy layers and smelled faintly of sheep. Maybe she was a quilter or a basket weaver? Or—

Soap, I decided with a nod. That had to be it. She was here to make beautiful, scented soaps molded into the shapes of flowers and fawns and woodland mushrooms.

Having made up my mind about Soap Girl, I turned in the other direction. My eyes connected immediately with those of another teenage girl. She'd taken a step back from the circle and she was clearly sizing me up.

I gave her a cringey smile.

Caught me, I mouthed.

She laughed and headed toward me.

Or should I say, she wafted toward me. Everything about this girl was light and fluttery, from her long black hair—a cascade of glossy, tight ringlets—to her blowsy, ankle-skimming skirt. Her skin wasn't just brown—it was brown with golden undertones. The girl practically glowed.

When she reached me, she gave me a mischievous smile.

"You were totally judging that girl over there, weren't you?" she said.

"Um," I stammered. "I think judging is kind of a harsh way to put it, but. . ."

"What class do you think she's taking?" the girl asked.

"Soapmaking," I said quickly. "Definitely soapmaking."

"See?" she said, a gleeful bubble in her voice. "You're wrong. I asked her a few minutes ago and she's taking canning."

"Canning?"

"Oh, it's a new class Camden added," the girl said with a graceful flick of her hand. "You know, jams, jellies, pickles. Anything you can put in a jar. I'm from New York and it's the thing up there. You can't throw a rock without hitting somebody in a slouchy hat carrying a box of mason jars. And probably a messenger bag full of bacon. Not that I would ever."

"Throw a rock at somebody?" I asked. I was kind of having a hard time following this girl. For somebody who looked so zen and wispy, she sure talked fast.

"Or eat bacon," she replied. "Anyway, I'm Annabelle. I'm taking pottery."

Of course you're taking pottery, I thought, suppressing a giggle. But what I said out loud was, "Oh, cool. Pottery's fun."

"Oh, it's more than fun," she said. Then she launched into an explanation of her choice, talking so excitedly that I could only make out a few snatched phrases.

"I need to live before I head to college in the fall . . . reach deep into my inner being . . . suck the marrow out of life . . . not just a taker, you know, but a maker . . . I'm taking pottery as a way to get back to the earth . . ."

When she seemed to be done with her monologue—which had more twists and turns to it than a mountain road, I smiled, nodded hard and said, "That's great! You go!"

Luckily, Annabelle didn't see my vague response for what it was: I have no idea what you just said.

Instead, she'd clasped her hands in front of her chest and looked a bit misty-eyed as she said, "Thank you for that validation. Really."

"Um, no problem," I said. "By the way, I'm Nell."

"No. Way," Annabelle said, her dark eyes widening. I noticed that her lashes were as lush and curly as her hair.

"Yes, Nell," I sighed. "I know it must sound like a hopelessly hillbilly name, especially to someone from New York. My family. . ."

"Nell," Annabelle said with a frown. "First of all, never apologize for your name. Your name is an essential part of your identity. Second of all, if you're Nell Finlayson, you're my roommate!"

I blinked.

"Well, I am Nell Finlayson," I said, "so I guess I am. Your roommate I mean."

As I said this, I felt a mixture of excitement and panic.

Annabelle clearly had what adults called a "strong personality." The thing is, I'm pretty sure the adults hardly ever mean that as a compliment.

"So, Nell, how old are you?" Annabelle demanded bluntly.

"Fifteen," I said.

"I'm two years older than you," she replied. "Which means, I'm in a position to give you some advice."

"More advice, you mean?" I said, before I could stop myself.

Annabelle didn't seem to notice. Instead she looped her arm through mine. We were about the same height, five foot seven, but next to her willowy goldenness, I felt washed out and shriveled. Her clothes were a rippling rainbow of plum and teal, mustard and aqua. Meanwhile, my skinny capris were dark gray and my tank top was the brooding color of an avocado peel. My hair— freshly blunt cut and flatironed to a crisp—was dyed black. Only my feet had a bit of brightness to them. I was wearing my favorite, acid-yellow, pointy-toed flats.

"Check out that," Annabelle ordered me. She pointed at the disembodied fiddle bow, which was still doing its little dance in the center of the crowd.

I glanced at it, then shrugged at Annabelle.

"I'm not talking about the instrument," Annabelle insisted. She grabbed me by the shoulders and shuffled me sideways until we were able to peek through a break in the crowd. "I'm talking about the player!"

I followed her gaze to the musician

And then I caught my breath.

The fiddler was a boy.

A boy who was clearly in high school. (His cut-off khakis, orange-and-green sneakers, and T-shirt that said, ASHWOOD HIGH SCHOOL CROSS COUNTRY were a hint.)

I might have also noticed that the boy's eyes were a deep, beautiful blue. You could see the color even though he was wearing glasses with chunky, black frames. His glossy, dark brown hair flopped over his forehead in a particularly cute way. His nose had just a hint of a bump in the bridge and I could tell that his torso was long and slim beneath his faded yellow T-shirt.

And, oh yeah, his playing was beautiful, too. Maybe even a notch above boring. His style was studied, sure. His rhythms were too even and his transitions were too careful to be untrained. He was clearly one of those Practicers that Nanny had always wanted me to be (but that I never had been).

But he also had talent.

No, more than that—he had The Joy.

The Joy makes you play until your fingertips are worn with deep, painful grooves.

The Joy makes you listen to all 102 versions of Hallelujah until you can decide which interpretation you love the best, even if it drives the rest of your family crazy.

And The Joy makes your face contort into funny expressions as you play.

I couldn't help but notice that, even while this boy was grimacing and waggling his eyebrows during the climax of his song, he still looked pretty good.

And when he stopped playing? When his thick eyebrows settled into place, his forehead unscrunched and his pursed lips widened into a smile while the crowd applauded for him?

Well, then, he became ridiculously good looking.

"See what I'm talking about?" Annabelle said.

I opened my mouth and closed it again. How could I tell Annabelle that, even if he was really, really good-looking, I could never be interested in someone who'd so clearly drunk the Camden Kool-Aid.

If I said that, I'd basically be insulting everybody who was there, including her.

So I just shrugged, and said, "Um, yeah, nice fiddling."

"Nice?! That was lovely." Nanny had appeared at our sides. "That young man had better be in our class."

"Our class?" Annabelle inquired, blinking inquisitively at my grandmother.

"Nanny, this is Annabelle," I said. "We just figured out that we're roommates."

I turned back to Annabelle. "My grandma is one of Camden's fiddle teachers."

"And Nell is going to be my assistant," Nanny said proudly.

"Uh, yeah," I confirmed, trying not to sound morose.

Annabelle looked from me to Nanny then back to me.

"Interesting," she said.

Then she glanced at the dispersing circle of music lovers.

"And, hmm, I think it's about to get even more so."

"Huh?" I said.

I followed her gaze to the fiddler. This time, he was the one staring—with wide eyes and a sudden blush on his neck—at me!